LUCAS

Elna Holst

A NineStar Press Publication

Published by NineStar Press
P.O. Box 91792,
Albuquerque, New Mexico, 87199 USA.
www.ninestarpress.com

Lucas

Printed in the USA
First Edition
April, 2020

Print ISBN: 978-1-951880-88-0

Also available in eBook, ISBN: 978-1-951880-86-6

Warning: This book contains sexually explicit content, which may only be suitable for mature readers, description of stillbirth, and mention of past non-consensual sexual abuse.

I thought ease would come, here, tucked away in the safe uneventfulness of Hunsford. It would seem I was mistaken.

In 1813, upon her marriage to Mr Collins, the rector of Hunsford Parsonage, Charlotte Collins *née* Lucas left her childhood home in Hertfordshire for Kent, where she is set to live out her life as the parson's wife, in an endless procession of dinners at Rosings Park, household chores, correspondence, and minding her poultry. But Mrs Collins carries with her a secret, a peculiar preference, which is destined to turn all her carefully laid plans on their head.

Lucas is a queer romance, a mock-epistolary novel, and a retelling and continuation of Jane Austen's *Pride and Prejudice*, teeming with Regency references and Sturm und Drang. It is an homage to English literature—and a brazen, revisionist fan fiction. But, first and foremost, it is a love story. Read it as you will.

My heartfelt gratitude goes out to A Lady, Samuel Richardson, Mrs Radcliffe, Miss Maria Edgeworth, as well as Currer, Ellis and Acton Bell, without whose shining examples the following pages might never have been committed to paper.

Heiligenschwendi, near Thun
February, 1852

Darling Izzie,

Enclosed you will find some old papers of my aunt's—my twice dead aunt!—of the queerest nature. I trust you to burn them before you so much as read a line of them, for that was my downfall. My papa would have them burnt, and as you know, his directions must be followed. Luckily, he did not suspect the exact contents of my aunt's escritoire, or he would have never trusted me with the office.

My dear, these *belles lettres*, as we may call them, are really too shocking for words. More shocking even than that vile rake Cleland's effusions; for, as we know, that is <u>but</u> fiction, whereas, this! I blush to think on the likely veracity of these incendiary epistles. As you shall see—but I forget myself, you shall not see. You must burn everything at once, even this, my prefatory note, for if my papa or your mamma were to find out— Well!

I long to see you, dear. Switzerland is rather dreary and dull this time of year, which, come to think of it, England is, too, but it has the decided advantage of your companionship. I am eager, very eager, to return and be once more.

Your faithful and ever loving,

Lottie

Volume One

Hunsford Parsonage
September, 1815

Dear Lizzy,

I was a wretch today.

I woke up with a pain in my face, which collected into a dull, thudding sort of pang over my left eyebrow. It seemed to herald ill news, and I dreaded a note from you at breakfast, bearing tidings of the worst. There was none, of course. Of course. Good Lord.

There. Now you know what a strange mood I was in. You would be surprised at your old, sensible friend Charlotte writing in so nonsensical a manner, but then, you will never receive this. I always write another letter after the first.

Do you know I started writing these missives to you when you were but a girl of fifteen? It began just after the day in the garden at Longbourn when you told me that dream of yours. It was mid-September then, as it is now, and the gaiety of the new autumnal colours about us fairly scorched my eyes. I was prone to the occasional headache even at nineteen, though I was at pains to conceal them, lest this weakness should further lessen my chances of securing an eligible match. I was dressed in my leafy-green woollen gown, and you were in a pale yellow muslin, defying nature as is your wont, your shivers exposing your budding womanly features through the delicate material.

Surely, you must remember? I remember everything about that day in sharp, agonising detail.

"My dear Charlotte," you said at length, and your voice held a note of supplication, of hesitancy, which was out of character for you. "I had the oddest dream tonight, and I feel I must tell it, although I fear you will think the worse of me for doing so. And yet it lingers, and I must have it out if ever I am to be at my ease!"

You laughed and shivered afresh, and a branch of rowan berries danced in the wind behind you. I took your cold hand in my lap and entreated you to go on, saying something feeble and high-minded about how I would not judge you for the world—or something along an equally sentimental strain, which I squirm to recollect.

"You are too good to me, Charlotte. You always were. Between you and Jane, I shall grow up to become the most insufferable of creatures. No, I see what you are about to say—" And you held up your free hand to quell my protestations. On account of the autumnal air, we were seated so close to each other that your fingers were a hair's breadth from brushing my lips.

I was blushing; I can write that here. I was undone, even before you told me the contents of your dream.

And then you did.

*

Mr Collins has interrupted me, which is just as well. He came to reproach me once more, before bedtime, on my impertinent conduct at Rosings Park. I am not perturbed. His displeasure will, I fear, pass more quickly than my own complaint.

I have so much to tell you, yet words fail me, or—as you see—tumble out of me in a flow of inconsistencies. I was writing about your dream, but I need not go into that, or I shall have little chance of a quiet night—and then I will be wretched on the morrow as well.

Suffice it to say it brought on the habit of penning these unsent letters to you, for 'I must have it out', as you put it, 'if ever I am to be at ease!'

I thought ease would come, here, tucked away in the safe uneventfulness of Hunsford. It would seem I was mistaken. But more to come.

Hunsford Parsonage
September, 1815

Good morning, my dear Eliza,

It is a good morning, and I feel I have regained some of my equilibrium. There was a letter from Pemberley at breakfast today, and you are all very well. You have not been laid up yet, but I can tell from the impatient twirls of your *p's* that it must happen soon. I hope there will not be a great deal of pain. In my letter to you now, I was on the point of enclosing a receipt for a draught which the old nurse here was so good as to impart to me when I was in that way, but I decided against it.

You see, I have grown quite superstitious. None of my misfortune must be allowed to taint your future happiness.

Instead, I described the autumn litter of baby rabbits outside my window. Their likenesses to some of our shared acquaintance must divert you, I think. My husband has gone into his garden in the hopes, I doubt not, of catching Miss de Bourgh passing in her carriage, so that he may offer the proverbial olive branch &c.

He is most decidedly vexed. At breakfast, he spoke hardly above two sentences put together to me, which for him is as close to taciturn as he is ever likely to venture. It was, therefore, quite a pleasant repast, and I had leisure not only to read your letter but to speak to Travis about the leg of mutton she has had her eye on for us. William's countenance softened at this exchange; Travis's lamb stew is one of his favourite dishes of the season, though he would be loath to admit it could hold its own to the dry and overcooked meals we are habitually served at the Park.

Lady Catherine's palate must have grown indifferent over the years. How her daughter and Mrs Jenkinson put up with it, I confess, I do not know. It is a testament, I suppose, to the utter inefficacy of gainsaying the lady of the house.

But I am prevaricating, and if you were in reality to receive this, you would be upbraiding me. So, let us return to, and then forever be done with, the subject of last night at Rosings Park.

In my defence (and I must be allowed to defend myself to you, Eliza), I had, at regular intervals during the day, pleaded with my husband to be spared from going. Naturally, he would have none of it, and the frequency of his visits to my chambers to ascertain if I had not, after all, made some recovery, irked me to the point where I at last professed myself to be quite equal to attending her ladyship's dinner party, merely for the relief of being left a few hours to myself.

I was not well. My reflection stared back at me from the looking glass with hollow eyes, ghostly cheeks—even my hair appeared wan and affected. I dreaded spending an evening under the scrutiny of Lady Catherine; she has little patience for anyone's sickliness but her daughter's, and that, too, fails her at times. My sole consolation was that it was Thursday and so Dr Reid, our village physician, would be one of the party. In my misery, I fancied that the good doctor might have some drops of laudanum about his person, which he could slip me, quietly, between paper-dry pheasant and undercooked quail eggs. How bewildering are the fitful hopes of the indisposed!

At the appointed hour, I entered the hall at Rosings on my husband's arm, cross as a child dragged out of bed after but two hours of rest, and there indeed was Dr Thomas Reid, and with him a lady whom I had never set eyes on before.

"Mr and Mrs Collins," the footman announced, and Lady Catherine's head turned abruptly from her conversation with the wraithlike creature.

As we drew closer I noted that despite her pallid complexion the stranger had a fine head of natural curls, simply, yet skilfully, arranged in a style which has gone out of fashion some fifteen years since. My curiosity was roused, notwithstanding my distemper.

"Miss Reid, allow me to introduce to you our rector, Mr Collins, and his wife, Mrs Collins. Miss Reid is the cousin of Dr Reid, lately joining him from the family estate in G___."

My husband bowed low in the woman's general direction, then concerned all his mental faculties with paying his respects to our ever-obliging hostess. My face warmed.

"Miss Reid, I am very pleased to make your acquaintance. Your journey must have been a long and tedious one. How long have you been in Kent?"

No doubt, Lizzy, you would have taken my inane repetition of the word 'long' as proof of my confusion. You would not have been mistaken. On the spur of the moment, without bethinking myself, I offered her my hand, which she grasped readily enough. I was surprised, considering her ephemeral appearance, by its strength. It was warm and steadfast: a good, kind, capable sort of hand. Looking up, I was met by a pair of eyes which positively glowed.

"Mrs Collins, the pleasure is all mine. Dear Tom has spoken highly of you and of Hunsford. I have not been here long."

"Ailsa—Miss Reid—" The doctor cut in. "—that is to say, I had the great pleasure of receiving word from my cousin that she was to join me here but a fortnight ago. She arrived a week later, but has, unfortunately, been very ill from her travels."

I looked at our esteemed physician, flustered and with a stiffened jaw, and could all too well make out his meaning. Miss Reid was not, in his opinion, well enough for company, but the inevitable visit to Rosings could not be further postponed.

My hand, which still gripped Miss Reid's, could not forbear pressing it in commiseration. Her radiant gaze met mine, and the smile she gave me warmed me in the most unaccountable way.

Regrettably, Mr Collins here found his cue to turn the poor woman's precarious health into a ham-fisted excuse for complimenting his patroness.

"To be sure, Miss Reid," my spouse ejaculated, "you will not find a better constitutional than to dine at Rosings Park. Lady Catherine—"

And he was off. Reluctantly, I let go of the hand I had held too long already, and turned to, if at all possible, lessen the prolificacy of my husband's folly. I hastened to direct his attentions back to our hostess, whose subsequent oratory on the insipid intrepidness of today's young ladies, dashing hither and thither across the country without a thought as to what the inclemency of our weather might do to our necessarily more delicate constitutions—at this juncture, she broke off to tell me I was looking very gloomy myself this evening—would not be abated until dinner was announced.

*

The dinner itself was a miserable affair. My headache made me peevish, and I was impatient to escape the clutches of Lady de Bourgh's ponderous and offensive intercourse. You are no stranger to this sentiment, Eliza, and I know you have always looked upon my forbearance with it with a mixture of admiration and disgust.

I know you have been disgusted with me. How could it be otherwise?

As ever, Lady Catherine took what seemed a particular delight in criticising her new acquaintance. More than once I chanced to catch Dr Reid's temples reddening with held-back anger and mortification.

I could not but mirror his emotion.

Miss Reid bore the onslaught with a quiet composure, however: one which I suspect had more to do with her present state of feverishness than a meek and angelic disposition. So much the better. Angels are routinely picked to pieces by Lady Catherine de Bourgh.

"But who is your father?" cried her ladyship at one point, exasperated by the dullness of her companions.

"My father and mother died when I was but a small child," replied Miss Reid calmly, and I inwardly applauded her, even as I was vexed to see the minute signs of her growing distress. "I was brought up at my father's brother's estate in G__ together with Tom and our cousin, my uncle's son. We were like brothers and sister."

Here she glanced at Dr Reid—Tom, I could not help thinking—and there was such a co-mingling of sensations in her countenance, such a patchwork of fondness, chagrin, and perplexity, I felt desperate to lure the shrew's attention away from her.

"Lady Catherine," I said, and in an instant my mouth went dry; my mind gave way to a tabula rasa. Her ladyship's lips crinkled into a tight rosebud of disapproval. Casting about for a topic, I turned to the only—if meagre—support I had.

William's eyes were clouded over, his jowls trembling. I could have kicked him in frustration.

"Mr Collins tells me that you have plans for planting a grove of alder trees at the north-east of the park. What an ingenious addition to the beautification of your grounds that will be."

On hearing myself repeat my husband's speech from the day before last, verbatim, I mentally flinched at my perfect mimicry of his supercilious intonation. William dabbed at his mouth with his napkin. This was familiar territory to him—thank Heaven! His ensuing praise of her ladyship's scheme, taste, refinement, savoir-faire—in short, of everything but her red velvet shoes, which tapped the floor furiously at the interruption—kept the party occupied till well into dessert.

Dr Reid lifted his wine glass to me in a silent toast. I drank and coloured like a naughty maid.

*

Well, my dear Elizabeth, what is your verdict? Now that it is daylight, the morning sun falling pleasantly through the window to adorn my writing desk with warming shafts of yellow, I am taken aback only by my own unhappy consternation. But I am not in pain today.

I dare say Mr Collins's pique will wear off by and by. Although his intuition tells him that her ladyship was not altogether satisfied with me last night, his limited reason prevents him from seeing precisely wherein lay my faux pas. The impudence of my, at any occasion, interrupting Lady Catherine he feels most keenly, but as for my introduction of a subject which must in every respect be such an agreeable one—that, he can never find fault with.

No more of this. Your interest would certainly lie in the further welfare and whereabouts of our regular practitioner and his mysterious cousin, and on that head I can offer no intelligence, either to you, my half-imaginary bosom friend, or to myself. I cannot say. Has she indeed taken up residence with him? For how long is she to stay at Hunsford? Will we have the opportunity of seeing her again?

In my proper letter to you, I abbreviated this whole erratic confessional into a prosaic: 'We made a new acquaintance at Rosings last night, a Miss Reid of G___, cousin of Dr Reid.' I long for you to ask me about her, so that I may, in a second letter, write: 'She seems a very pleasant sort of girl. I hope to be better acquainted with her.'

Hunsford Parsonage
September, 1815

Dear Lizzy,

It is really ridiculous that I should have been so put out of my way by Thursday night at Rosings. And pitiful, poorly looking Miss Reid! What is it to me if Dr Reid brings six and twenty female cousins to reside with him?

I am glad propriety led me to curtail my mention of the matter in my genuine correspondence with you. How silly I feel now that three days have passed since that fated evening. What business had I to throw myself in the way of Lady C.? I have done nothing but cause fretfulness in my husband and upset the tranquil state of affairs in my own household.

I suppose there is still that in me which longs for the comforts of a female companion. You know I have chosen my situation in life with open eyes. I confess that there was also something, something perverse and self-chastising, about my desire to take myself safely out of your immediate reach. And yet how it has weighed on me, this reserve that sprung up between us upon my announcement of my impending marriage. But Lizzy, how could I have acted differently? How could I have sat quietly at Lucas Lodge, observing first-hand as Mr D. fell ardently in love with you? You could not understand me. You cannot understand me. I imagine the only one who could ever hope to understand me would be Mr D. himself.

I do like him. He is exactly and precisely everything I could have wished for you. To behold the shimmer of happiness upon you as you look at him sends me into an ecstasy of elation, pain, and jealousy—

Oh, my pen is running away with me. As I write this, my left hand is clutching for support, fretting at the small bronze key hidden inside the confines of my stays, where it hangs from a long, thin riband around my neck. I lock these 'letters' away, you see. Of course I do. The ones I have not burnt. It would be better for me to cease my scribblings and burn the lot. Still I have held on to them, too many of them, for ten years. Why will you not let go of me, Lizzy? Why will I not let go of you?

In a few months, I shall be thirty years of age. You will be the mother of not one but two small children. I am not sure how that should bring me peace. As I tend the grave of my little Henry, I am not sure if there will ever be peace to be had.

*

Travis just in with a note from Miss Reid. She wishes to be better acquainted with me. She desires me to take tea in the village.

*

Eliza—I am this moment back from the doctor's, and I have my poultry to attend to, preparations for Mr Collins's evening meal to make. I have not the time to sit here, dumbfounded, dripping ink staining my fingertips. And yet I must tell you, though I know not how. The change, the utter reversal of Miss Reid! But perhaps I am mistaken—do I say change? Did I not detect something about her person from the start?

I am not making sense. This calls for a proper account. Until night-time then, we shall have to wait!

*

Now. I have just seen Mr Collins to his bedchamber. It ought to be the other way around, I dare say, but we do not stand upon formalities at Hunsford Parsonage. Oh, I am giddy as a girl. Even William is appeased by my change of demeanour. I should take care. Tomorrow he may propose accompanying me to my chambers—but propitiously, he has the visit from the Archdeacon to prepare for, and I must caution him against additional exertions, lest he should be in danger of disappointing Lady C. with being overfatigued for her Tuesday game of cards.

I should be ashamed of myself. But not tonight.

I arrived at Dr Reid's house, which is just off the main road, at a little before one o'clock. I was in my best woollen gown, the mauve one with fine silk trimmings, which you pressed upon me as a gift on our excursion to Bath the winter before last. You will remember it but too well. It was less than a month after we lost H. and despite my genuine gratitude at your concern and affection, I have not been able to wear it since. The memories, yes—but also, there has been little occasion. We did not go to Meryton for Christmas last year, and it is certainly too smart for any visit to Rosings Park. I would not have it dolefully sneered at by the inhabitants of that house.

Be all that as it may, I felt a little uneasy, unused to be in my fineries, as I knocked at the door at Dr R.'s.

Promptly, as if he had been standing right on the other side of it, the door was opened by the manservant, who informed me that the doctor was out.

I struggled to conceal my confusion. "I did not—that is, I had an invitation to take tea with Miss Reid?"

"James!" A voice came from within. "Is that Mrs Collins? For Heaven's sake, do not keep her standing without in the cold!"

An energetic woman of indistinguishable age elbowed said James in his midsection in her hurry to bustle me into the house.

James stepped forlornly aside.

"Pay him no heed, Mrs Collins. The man has not adjusted to my mistress being part of the household yet. He is ever so set in his ways."

The stout maidservant had a shock of wild, speckled curls barely kept in place by a white cap, and a broad Scots accent, which I found surprisingly pleasing to the ear. The familiarity of her manners should have provoked my censure; my husband, I know, certainly would have fallen into a frenzy of convoluted reprobations, and maybe even yours, my dear Eliza, for all his condescending affability since your marriage took place, would not have stood for the unceremoniousness of Lilly.

I was charmed, with only a twitch of concern for our medical man's dutiful butler.

"Now, Mrs Collins, ma'am, if you please. Do make yourself comfortable in here in the drawing-room, and my lady shall be with you directly. She has just had her afternoon nap, you see—her cousin's orders!"

"Oh, but I did not mean to inconvenience her. If I had known I should not have arrived so early. I will take a walk about the village and return in half an hour."

I swerved on my heels towards the door again. The maid spun me back towards the drawing-room.

"You will do no such thing, Mrs Collins. My mistress explicitly— Why, here she is now!"

Twisting my head to look in the direction the good-humoured, but stubborn maid indicated, my eyes caught on Miss Reid coming downstairs.

This part gives me pause, Lizzy. For I hardly know how to describe her appearance to do justice to her transformation. My respect for Dr Reid's professional powers fairly shot through the roof.

For there, truly, was Miss Reid, stepping down the stairs. After but three days since last I saw her, she was a changed creature. Her cheeks glowed with the freshness of youth and returning health. Her eyes, when they alighted upon me, sparkled like newly shined plate. Her soft, pink lips parted in a friendly smile that promised... I cannot say. I was overcome with a turmoil of emotions. As discreetly as I could, I steadied myself against the doorpost, and the Scotswoman spoke in my stead:

"Oh, but you do look well, Ma'am! Does she not, Mrs Collins? These rests which dear Master Reid prescribes are doing wonders for your complexion, my lass. Soon you will look quite yourself again."

"Lilly, you forget yourself." Miss Reid spoke scoldingly, yet so sweetly that the spirited servant could hardly take offence. "Mrs Collins, pray do forgive my maidservant's freedoms; she has cared for us since I and Tom were but colts in sheep's clothings, and I am afraid she looks upon us as quite her own."

"Nonsense!" said Lilly. "I have treated Mrs Collins with nothing but the utmost respect."

"Oh! Yes," I broke in, as I had become mistress of my own voice at last, and did not wish to be the cause of any discord in that house. "Your maid has been very obliging to me. She is very kind. Though I must beg your pardon, I would have called at a later hour had I known I would arrive at such an inopportune moment."

Miss Reid shook her head and laughed, her pretty locks of hair dancing about her in a way which renewed my confusion. Lilly smiled and looked at me with approbation. I had the notion, I know not whence, that it had been a while since she had had the pleasure of hearing her mistress laugh.

Miss Reid came towards me, her hands extended to take mine.

"This will not do. We must lay aside our excuses for the present. My object is not to let you out of this house until we have become the best of friends, and at this rate, we shall not have made any progress past the common formalities before Michaelmas. Do step across that threshold you are loitering at, Mrs Collins, and let us issue a universal pardon to one another, and to Lilly and James, and to my cousin's tempestuous cock outside, for the remainder of the day."

*

The drawing-room at Dr Reid's is a snug, comfortable sort of room, though rather on the smallish side. What it lacks in size, it amply makes up for in a vast assortment of curiosities lining the shelves along the walls on all sides. There are trinkets from faraway places, shells and feathers, and vials of sand and dirt. But there is also chirurgical paraphernalia, and boxes with forbidding labels, such as femurs, phalanges, fibulas, and tibias. And there are glass jars.

"Don't look too closely, Mrs Collins, if you are the squeamish sort." Miss Reid's voice came from behind me, and there was amusement in it, but also something else. A challenge?

"This is an impressive collection," I observed, keeping my tone even. "I did not know the doctor had such a predilection for curios."

"Nor did I!" Miss Reid admitted, and her pearly laughter washed over the back of my neck like the sea surf. I placed my hand over my neck, stupidly, to stem the tide rising within me in response.

"Dear Tom always did collect an array of wild and wonderful natural objects when we were children—it was for his studies, he used to say—but I had no notion that he had kept up the habit since he grew into manhood. What a cabinet of wonders this poor drawing-room has become! I have to tell you, Mrs Collins, sometimes I despair of him ever finding a suitable wife."

I turned to look at her. A terrible premonition beset me— Terrible, I know not why. But to think...

"He is not eight and twenty, with a laudable profession and a comfortable home."

"Indeed," agreed Miss Reid, a humorous glint in her eye. "But what woman would put up with this? Could she be a sensible sort? Could she be sound of mind? She must be a very peculiar cast of female, to be sure."

"Someone…" I blushed at my presumption, yet it would out. "Someone like yourself, perhaps, Miss Reid?"

She looked startled. Then she broke into that rapturous merriment anew, and this time, Lizzy, I allowed myself the luxury of being swept up by it, of letting it enter and infect me until I was warmed and tingling from head to toe. What harm could it do?

"Oh! Mrs Collins," she spluttered, when she had regained control of herself. "You divert me exceedingly. I knew you would. But you are mistaken, grievously so, if you think I came here in pursuit of a husband who is as good as a brother to me. Marry Tom? I love him dearly, you know—but never, never! I am not, I fear, the marrying kind. Will you sit down, Mrs Collins?"

I sat. I think I would have jumped through the window if she had asked me to do so, such was the strange power her presence exerted over me; such was my befuddled relief at her denial of any matrimonial intentions on her part where Dr Reid was concerned.

Never, never. Miss Reid stood over me for a moment, affording me a better view of her features than I had hitherto been privy to. She is a fine, handsome girl. Despite the slenderness of her limbs, there is an impression of strength and tenacity about her, now that the last shreds of her indisposition have fallen away. She was wearing a poplin frock in a powdery shade of lilac that perfectly complemented my own mauve wool. She was the light shade to my darker one. She sighed, as if to clear herself of the last remnants of laughter, and as the top of her chest lifted with the inhalation, I had to resort to pinching myself not to swoon.

You have seen me pinch myself on occasion before, I dare say. Oh! What is to become of me, Eliza? What am I to do?

*

I left Dr Reid's but an hour later. There had been tea, and crumpets, and small gherkin sandwiches. I know not the particulars. All I know is that by the time I left, the sly, infinitely engaging creature had extracted from me a promise that she should be allowed to call me by my Christian name whenever we are in private. Such precipitousness would shock you, I am sure. It shocks me. It shocks me to the core of my being. And she—dear, shocking, prepossessing Miss Reid—is to be Ailsa, Ailsa to me.

Hunsford Parsonage
September, 1815

Dearest Eliza,

A note from Pemberley this morning and you are well, wonderfully well. Your little Jane has been born, and by your description—short, but full of the new mother's blossoming admiration for her child—I take it that she has every mark of health and longevity upon her. From what you tell me, even her brother, Fitz, seems enamoured, which is no mean feat. I congratulate you from the bottom of my heart. I shall do so in my formal letter to you also, and you will, I expect, or rather your husband will, have the doubtful pleasure of receiving William's effusions upon the subject. Telling him of the impropriety of addressing himself on such an occasion to such a man, who must be his superior in every sense of the word, is as you know too well, Lizzy, to no avail. I comfort myself that you will teach Mr D. to laugh at the matter. Your familial felicity could not be rattled by twenty Mr Collinses.

And I pray, do not let any imagined grief on the part of one Mrs Collins cloud your joy in your secondborn. I am well. I am relieved. My only dread was that you, my darling Eliza, would be afflicted with the same sorrow that I have had to bear. And yet, I know that the loss of an infant is nothing out of the common way.

I am so wearied by the common way.

When I went down to his little grave today I discovered a rosebud there. Where could anyone have come by rosebuds at this time of the year? And, more to the point, who? Perhaps the old nurse who tended me... But really, she must have seen tenscore children lost since my Henry. Travis? She likes me well enough, I am sure, but there is not that cordiality or level of informality between us that might induce a servant to visit the resting place of her mistress's stillborn child. My husband?

Would that it were William. Perchance it could reconcile me to the thought of letting him into my bed again. But perversely, the thought of bearing another child is abhorrent to me. At times, as I close my eyes, I can feel the weight of my dead babe in my arms. His waxen, birdlike limbs cooling too soon. His little hands that will never grab for me, never implore me, and yet which hold my heart so much the firmer in their lethal impotence.

The mauve frock hangs where I left it, on the door of my closet. What induced me to wear it? It shames me to think what frivolous thrills I experienced in it only the day before last. And all the while, you lay in labour, and I—

*

Tuesday night. We have been to the card tables at Rosings. I shall let you know more by and by.

*

Wednesday morning. As I suspected, the physician and his cousin had been invited to join us for cards at Rosings Park last night. Lady C.'s rapacity for quadrille has her issuing invitations to the unlikeliest of opponents.

And her curiosity as to Miss Reid's provenance was, after all, by no means stilled by Thursday's ill-fated dinner party.

I could not but smile at her ladyship's unfeigned astonishment at Ailsa's improved looks. She was positively shining last night, Lizzy. And once more, quixotically, our gowns were strangely, unaccountably well-matched: she in yellow cambric with white lace trimmings, I in a gold robe of India muslin with black embroidered frills.

She is utterly beguiling. Now that her strength is back, she holds her own to Lady Catherine. But no, I am making too light of it. It is completely unprecedented, and I fear you would not call my judgement entirely sound upon the matter, but it seems she has managed not merely to subdue her ladyship, but, truthfully, to have charmed her.

William is out of his depth. Whereas his depraved profusions of flattery have always worked peculiarly well to curry favour from the Lady's narrow-minded egotism, Miss Reid's youthful beauty and wry Scottish wit has, incongruously, in the space of an evening, turned all the attentions of his patroness unto herself.

He is not best pleased. For my part, I have never understood the good lady better.

As we parted for the evening, I had worked up the courage to ask Ailsa, Miss Reid, to call on me on the morrow. I fear my voice was hushed and stuttering, verging on the pathetic, as I made my request.

She smiled and professed she should like nothing better.

And so I left on Mr Collins's arm, feeling, in that instant, like the belle of the ball. Or like a suitor. I know not which.

*

Wednesday night. She has come and she has gone. I have had her here, under my own roof, in the sitting-room, which as you know, dear Eliza, I may more or less call my own.

I tremble as I write, I see. I have not had a fire lit tonight, and there is a storm brewing. How forgetful and distracted I have become. But no, I will not lie, not to you, here, in these pages. I have kept my rooms frigid to drive away my easily chilled spouse. I wanted to be left alone, this night of all nights, as I sit shivering in my nightgown, stroking the bud of a rose.

She has come and she has gone. But let me begin where I left off.

I was in a fluster when I woke up this morning, and poor Travis, I will admit, had to bear the brunt of it. I ordered her to dust where no dusting was needed. I ordered her to cook up strange and fanciful dishes, which neither she nor I knew properly how to make. I wanted cake. I wanted little morsels of perfectly white fish. I wanted ambrosia and tea—Oh! The best of tea! Not that sharpish gruel Mr Collins favours. Everything in our household was wrong. *I* was wrong. I had changed my habit three times before breakfast.

Travis smiled and curtseyed and tried her best to please me. I wondered at her. Then, as I watched her forbearance, her knowing look, it dawned on me that she must needs think she knew the reason behind my fickle temper. She must think I am in that way again—at last.

I could have struck her. I wanted to fall about her neck and cry it out. Instead, I changed into my oldest, most ragged gown, and set about cleaning the sitting-room, after I had sent Travis out scouring the country for proper red apples and thick yellow cream.

Poor Travis. Poor me. I was in such a state.

Mr Collins, conveniently, was at church all morning, busy fawning over the newly arrived deacon. Between this august visitor and his patroness, he is prodigiously employed and lost to the world at present. So much the better. Barring Travis and the stable lad out back, Ailsa and I would have the place to ourselves. I could not have contrived it better. Apart from my headache, that is.

Oh! Lizzy, this contumacious pain! Do you remember how, as a child, I was wont to faint away whenever I was overwrought? How this ache could always be relied upon to make the best of times the worst of times? Perhaps you do not. It changed character, as I grew into womanhood. Once guard-napkins had become a regular stock of my wardrobe, the pangs that used to worry my mother that I was of a sickly constitution subsided, or nearly so, and I became the composed and dependable creature you all came to associate with 'dear Charlotte'. I learnt to conceal those eruptions which lingered (on you telling me about your dream—yes) and I cannot say where the more violent pangs slept for those years. But I can say that they returned with Henry—the blessing and bane of my life.

By the time Travis had returned and I was changing into my mauve wool for the second time in a week, my hands were shaking with agony.

"Would it not be better if we put you to bed, madam?" said she mildly, as I winced under her ministrations to my hair. "I am sure you are in no fit state to entertain any visitors. The doctor's lady friend will surely understand."

"Miss Reid is the doctor's cousin, Travis," I answered irritably, endeavouring not to look too hard at my greenish face in the mirror. "I beg you not to spread paltry and unfounded gossip in my house."

Travis flushed, but she was undeterred. She put a hand on my shoulder.

"You're not well, madam."

"I am perfectly well, thank you." I closed my eyes to fight back a wave of nausea. "At least I shall be. I simply need tea."

Travis's forehead furrowed. For a moment, I was concerned that she might see fit to apply to her master on the subject; but she knew as well as I that this could hardly produce a propitious result. She sighed and went to see about her tarts.

I gazed upon myself, pallid and pasty-faced, and began to waver. I have never been handsome, Eliza, and thus I have never been vain. And I so wished to see Ailsa, wished to have her in the same room as I, tête-à-tête, that I had not given a second thought to what effect my apparent malaise might have on her regard for me. I don't think even you, for all your stalwart friendship and genuine, generous affection, have ever ranked me among the local beauties. But this.

I pinched my cheeks hard enough to make tears spring to my eyes, but what little colour they could be teased into soon faded. I bit my lips. All in vain.

As I went downstairs, my heart sank with each step I took, and I knew Travis was right. I had to ask her to give Ailsa my excuses. I had to go back to bed.

I was too late.

As I came down the last stair, Travis was letting Ailsa in through the door, and our eyes met and it was like staring at the sun for too long; I saw blotches of colour, spots of light, and I fell, ignobly, back in a swoon.

The shame of it. I am not—I was not—a woman who swoons.

"Mrs Collins! Dear Mrs Collins— Excuse me, maid, will you send back for my cousin immediately?"

I came to, my head resting on velvet warmth—I could almost have fainted anew when I realised Ailsa had cushioned my head in her lap, her gloved hand stroking my hair away.

"No," I whispered. "No, no!"

"You are with us again. Thank Heaven! You gave us such a fright."

I sat up, steadying myself against the stairs.

"No physician, please."

Ailsa looked put out, charmingly so. I essayed a smile, but, I suspect, managed nothing more than a semblance of that reassuring facial expression.

"It is but a slight pain in my head. I was momentarily weakened. Please do not trouble yourself, Miss Reid. Travis—" I gazed up at my maidservant who was looking as miserable as I secretly felt. "Will you serve us tea in the sitting-room, please?"

"Travis will do no such thing," Ailsa interrupted, and there was a determined tilt to her chin, an air of authority and poise that forestalled any opposition I might venture to offer. "You will help me carry your mistress to her chambers; then you will brew some tea from some herbs which I shall supply."

I shook my head feebly, but that loathsome faintness was coming over me afresh. Ailsa put her hands under me, and I feared she might actually try to carry me up the stairs in her arms—such was her determination!

Her health having returned to her, she seems to have gained the vigour of a lioness.

"No, I—I can walk, if you will but give me your arm."

She relented. Between her and Travis, I was led back to my rooms, my feet barely skimming the floor.

As I lay against the pillows on my sofa, Ailsa brought out a small paper parcel from her reticule and handed it over to Travis, with instructions on how she should let the contents steep in boiled water and bring it back up to us presently. Travis's eyes flitted over to me, and I nodded. She curtseyed and was off.

"And now, Charlotte," Ailsa spoke pointedly. "Will you please explain yourself? Why would you not let me send for Tom?"

"Oh, Miss— Ailsa, I..."

She knelt by me, and my heart fluttered; my cheeks finally coloured of their own accord.

"It pains me to see you suffering so. Would you not be more comfortable in your bed?"

"I—I beg you will forgive me, Miss—Ailsa. I should not have let you see me indisposed. I am very sorry for it. I was on the point of asking Travis to give you my excuses, when—"

"Give me your excuses?" She looked horrified. "Why, I should have insisted on seeing you!"

Travis tapped on the door and brought in the tea tray. Ailsa inspected the light yellow liquid in the pot and commended her heartily. My maidservant's visage brightened.

"You can go back to your chores and let me tend to our patient, Travis. Rest assured she is in safe hands."

"Oh! Miss, will you not have some of the tart I prepared?"

Ailsa shook her head, smiling amiably.

"Mrs Collins cannot abide the smell of such delicacies at present, and I cannot abide leaving her side."

Travis inclined her head and closed the door on us.

"How came you to know?" asked I curiously, as I sat up and let Ailsa pour out the brew for us. It had a queer, but not unpleasant odour.

"You have a migraine. I have read about them in my uncle's library. We used to read together, Tom and I, before he went off to Edinburgh. I should have recognised it immediately, but I was distracted—" She put the delicate china cup in my hands, and held her own about mine, steadying them. "You must excuse me, Charlotte. I was too familiar with your servant, too familiar with you. I am afraid I was brought up quite wild, with no other women around than our sweet Lilly to teach me the ways of gentility. I try; goodness knows I try, but I cannot but look forever the impostor. I must rely on your tender heart, and your benign forbearance."

I felt weak, a delicious weakness that made me want to fall back against the cushions, to lie there indefinitely, and with such a nurse. Forbearance! To think that she should use that word. Forbearance is my weakness, not my strength. Forbearance is what makes me put up with Lady Catherine, pardon my husband's foibles, what makes me live so far away from...everything.

Her hands were still around mine as we lifted the cup to my lips, and I drank. The liquid contents of it had an acrid taste at first, but I did not mind. I could have drunk poison, gladly, if it had been administered thus. Ailsa took the cup from my hands and set it on its saucer. As she glanced back at me, I knew it was time for me to speak. But what could I say that would not break the enchantment? What could I say that would keep her by my side? I wet my lips.

"You're perfect," I said, and my voice broke. "You're a perfect gentlewoman to me."

A blush crept up her lovely countenance; but she did not look away. Instead, her darling hand touched my forehead, the soft skin of her wrist grazing my cheek, and there was a pulse there, unsteady, fitful, erratic—in perfect harmony with my own.

"You are too kind to me," she mumbled. "You make me— But you are not well, Charlotte. I forget myself. Will you allow me to rub your temples?"

I could not say no to her. I did not wish to.

She had me sit up, momentarily, as she removed my cap and took the place of my pillows in the seat next to mine. Then she made me recline anew, my head in her lap, so exquisitely close to her, as if I had been her newborn. As if I were hers. She put her hands around my head and pressed. I yelped.

"Oh! Your hairpins. You don't need these."

So saying, she pulled the pins Travis had been at such pains to arrange out of my hair, one after the other, and I should have been scandalised by her audacity, by the thought that my hair was falling free in her lap, but I could not have been disturbed by anything, Lizzy, even should she have stripped me down to the bone. I would have welcomed it.

Ailsa put the tips of her fingers to my temples, at the sides of my scalp, and as she rubbed in small, precise circles, blissful relief seemed to flow from them. I yawned contentedly. I closed my eyes. I drifted off.

When I awoke, the light had fallen outside. The tea tray had been removed, and I was lying with my head on the cushions of the sofa. There was no one in the room. I stretched languorously. My pain had subsided, but Ailsa had gone with it, and I was starting to worry that her presence here, the things she had said, the things she had made me feel, were all figments of a feverish imagination.

I put my hand to my head, tentatively, and found my hair loose. I put my hand to my chest and found... something. I picked it up and brought it to my lips, buried my nose in it, relishing its balmy, perfumy scent. It was a pink rosebud, the twin of the one I found on Henry's grave.

Hunsford Parsonage
September, 1815

Dearest Lizzy,

There was so much correspondence to get through this morning, I hardly had time to write to my secret friend. A letter from my sister Maria, detailing her receipt of our first communication from my sister Julia; as you know, she was lately married to one of the officers of the __shire Militia, a Mr Addison, who was once a fleeting favourite of Lydia's, I believe. Mrs Addison has been gone with her husband to join his new regiment in the East Indies these four months; her observations on her arrival at Nundydroog—which are just like her!—amount to little more than that the climate is hot, and the mosquitoes troublesome.

Maria assures me all is well in Meryton; your parents are preparing to travel into Derbyshire on the birth of their fourth grandchild, and my mother has begun to fear that there will never again be any eligible bachelors in that county to lead M. to the altar. My father proposes to convey them all to London for a change of scenery—an expense which their household could by no means sustain at present. Instead, Maria has suggested she should come here once the Bennets have returned from Derbyshire, that is, to prevent my mother wilting away from lack of company. Female company, we must assume, as there is no mention of my father having absented himself from Lucas Lodge.

I must, of course, acquiesce. I should like to see Maria, certainly. It is only— Well.

Also, there was a note from Dr Reid, thanking me—good Lord!—for the attention I have shewn his cousin, and wishing me a speedy recovery from my bout of 'hemicrania'. He hopes my husband will not be offended that he takes the liberty of writing directly to me, but as my physician he feels he must be allowed certain freedoms from the restrictions of the world at large.

He makes me laugh. I always liked our dear physician, but now that I know *her*, I like him infinitely more. I can hear *her* good sense echoed in his handwriting. I can see *her* standing behind him, advising him to forego inconsequential propriety. What a pair they are!

It would make sense... But it pains me even to write it. I seem to have lost all my wisdom on a certain lady's entering into Kent. All that is left is senselessness, strange and vague fancies, which I cannot begin to formulate to myself. In a few days, my husband shall be gone for a fortnight, travelling to Canterbury to pay his annual respects to the Archbishop. I do not know that this should really be necessary, but I encourage it; this year especially, with such vehemence that any other man might suspect his wife of purposely contriving to be rid of him.

Poor Mr Collins. I will have Travis wrap up a good quantity of that fruitcake he favours to see him on his way.

*

Thursday night. What an odd mixture of merriment and chagrin at Rosings tonight. Lady C. is not at all happy with the prospect of losing Mr Collins's simpering attentions for two weeks together, and had his itinerary not been so firmly settled, were it not that the coach leaves in the morning, I should not have put it past him to postpone his arrangements indefinitely. Her ladyship is of a fickle temperament, however. Only the week before last, she was urging him, most adamantly, to go.

The change is brought about, I would hazard to guess, by Miss de Bourgh's present listlessness. They are a very dull set at the moment. Mrs Jenkinson was looking quite put out.

So much for the chagrin, but the merriment, you ask? I must confess, I was, unbecomingly for a wife who is about to see her husband off on a journey, in very high spirits tonight. Ailsa and the doctor regaled me with anecdotes from their wild and wondrous childhood at G__, and I could not but laugh and smile, rather too freely for her ladyship's liking, I am afraid. They have invited me to go plum-picking with them at an orchard belonging to a farm a few miles north of here, and after some clever cajoling, Ailsa managed to persuade Lady Catherine that an outing might do her daughter and Mrs J. some good too. The lady herself, naturally, could never expose herself in such an outré fashion. I cannot think why Ailsa should wish Miss de Bourgh and Mrs Jenkinson to form part of the party, but she seems to pity the insipid woman, crushed like a fly under her mother's dictatorial thumb.

Hunsford Parsonage
October, 1815

He is off. I have the house to myself, and I am revelling in it. How nice it is to walk from room to room, and be certain, quite certain, that it is mine to dispose of as I see fit. It is like those innumerable hours we spent, one rainy summer, in the attics of Lucas Lodge. A kingdom of our own, where neither parents nor siblings, aunts or uncles, ever found us out. That consummate, if ephemeral feeling of being absolutely unfettered by society. How precious the memory of those summer months has been to me, Lizzy. How I have wished. How I have longed. How I have ached.

I did not send Travis off to seek out apples and cream today. I hoped *she* would come, but I had not durst suggesting it. Instead, I sat down to tea at my usual hour, the full flower of her rose in a crystal bowl adorning my table. I would content myself with this, I thought. I have no business constantly calling her away from Dr Reid.

And then there was a knock at the door, and it was as if my very chest had blossomed, a deep and grateful joy resounding in me; I heard her melodious voice asking Travis for my health; I heard Travis, uncommonly cheerful, saying she would announce her to me, and I sprang to my feet, sprang from the ground like a shoot, a bounce in my gait as I hastened to the door and burst through.

"You're here!"

Travis looked at me as if I had run quite mad. I suppose I have.

But there indeed was Ailsa, Miss Ailsa Reid, whose very name brings a thrill to my veins, spring to my heart in the midst of autumn.

She left Travis gawping behind her and approached me, a gentle smile on her face, shaking her head at my outburst. I could not be sorry. How often I have longed to be bold, Lizzy, to have... Here, at last, was my chance. I would not miss it.

"Charly," she said softly as she stood quite before me, her gloved hand mere inches from me. "Do go through to the sitting-room."

I backed across the threshold, and she came presently after, extending her arm to close the door behind us as we entered.

"Charly," she said again, her tone husky, her hand closing the gap to rest snug on my chest. "What will I do with you?"

I knew she could feel my heartbeat pounding against her palm. Surely, it spoke louder than any words could do? I hesitated. She let her hand drop.

"I did not mean to offend you." She lowered her head, her eyes hidden from me. "I take too many liberties, on such short an acquaintance. Only your family call you Charly, I dare say."

"No," I said, entangled in the odd broil of reactions from a moment ago, not quite trusting myself to speak, yet knowing I must; I should have spoken before. "That is to say, no one has ever called me Charly. They use Lotty as a term of endearment, betimes. But you are allowed to call me anything, anything at all."

She lifted her head, and her eyes were moist, a fine dew of tears quivering on her eyelashes. She wiped at them brusquely, grimacing.

I—I wanted to— I knotted my hands in my skirt.

"What was your name before marriage?" she asked, a hint of good humour returning to her features.

"Why, it was Miss Lucas. Miss Lucas of Lucas Lodge, eldest daughter of Sir William and Lady Lucas, at your service."

I mock bowed, playing the gallant to dry up the last of her tears, and with a forwardness I had not thought myself capable of, I took her hand and kissed it.

She gasped. I let go as if I had picked up a burning ember, but she shook her head violently, grasping my hand anew, pulling at it, pulling me towards her and—

Travis rapped at the door, calling out her "Tea, madam" an instant before opening it. We turned as one, away from each other, towards the table and chairs standing quite forgotten over by the window. For all the world—and to Travis, certainly—it must have looked as if we had quarrelled.

I sat, sensing rather than observing Ailsa take her place opposite me, my face aflame. Travis set down the tray which bore two slices of fruitcake and a pot of steaming green tea—the green tea I had insisted on her obtaining for Ailsa's last visit to this house. I peered up at her, and she gave me a little smile, curtseyed, and made to leave us.

Recovering myself, I called after her, "Thank you, Travis. Thank you."

"Certainly, madam," she replied, her tone warm as she closed the door.

I turned back to Ailsa and caught her petting one of the opened petals of my rose. Her rose. Our rose. She coloured prettily and said:

"Lucas. I should like to call you Lucas."

I picked up the teapot and served us both a good cupful of the scalding brew.

"Then Lucas I shall be."

She smiled and accepted her cup.

*

Saturday morning. We are off to the orchard today, in the nick of time, as the season is very nearly over. I have slept fitfully, my mind filled with a series of moving tableaux of Ailsa coming towards me, Ailsa's hand across my heart, tears in her eyes, and then—and then pulling me towards her, her eyes glistening, her lips— Could it be? Is it possible she feels—that—but I cannot! I cannot, even here... I must restrain myself. I have done so before. I can do so again.

But here is Travis climbing the stairs, Tom—Dr Reid—has arrived in his carriage to fetch me, no doubt, my key—

*

Saturday night. Oh, Eliza!

*

Sunday evening. I have had my last repast for the day; I have performed my ablutions; I have been to church where Mr Collins's understudy gave a commendably concise sermon. In passing, Ailsa has asked me if she may visit on the morrow, and I have said yes. A thousand times yes.

Dare I now, at this hour, sit and describe to you our outing of yesterday?

I have no choice. There is not a thing to distract me, no offices to be performed, no book of poetry or novel that can hold my attention, that can keep me from thinking, from reliving, again and again, like a pendulum clock stuck on chiming, chiming, chiming out the hour when—

We were an unexpectedly gay party on Saturday morning. Unexpectedly, I say, as the two ladies from Rosings joined us on route to the orchard in high spirits— nay, I may almost say in a state of elation. What would have been your impression, Eliza, if you had sat in the doctor's carriage with me, and had Mrs Jenkinson wave merrily at you as Miss de Bourgh's phaeton passed at a clipping speed?

But you were not in the carriage with me—Ailsa was. Sweet and mellow as the autumn sunlight about us, smiling and waving back, addressing me with an arched brow, a glint in her eye which I could not decipher.

"I expect her ladyship will be pleased with the effect of this excursion upon her daughter's humour, don't you?"

"It certainly seems that way," I mused. "I never—"

Ailsa shook her head and, with sudden emotion, clasped my hand.

"I know something about being a prisoner in a house which you cannot— But I mustn't upset you, not on a day like this. Some day, Lucas, I should like to tell you something about myself. I should like you to know...something about me. As yet, you must pardon me for holding back. I am not used to having friends."

She looked so in earnest, and a little pale, that I could not refrain from pulling the blanket we were sharing closer about her, from tilting my head towards her and whispering, "Lucas will always be your friend. You have won her over completely."

I thought— I thought she would, then, as the blood rushed in my ears: the intensity of that gaze! But Dr Reid swivelled in his seat, chuckling and chastising us for whispering about things we obviously thought were unfit for men's ears.

I would not blame him if he were jealous of his cousin's attentions. He seemed merely to be making an innocent jest, however, and we laughed politely and passed the time until our arrival in pleasant conversation. Under the blanket, Ailsa's fingers interlaced with my own, drawing lines and circles over the bridge of my hand that seemed to burn through the skin of my glove. If our medical man thinks the less of my intelligence after yesterday, I should not be surprised. But he is welcome to think me the greatest simpleton in the county of Kent, if he would but continue to drive me around said county, wrapped up with and caressed by his cousin, deliciously, tenderly tortured, while he requires me to give him my opinion on Dr Johnson, Mrs Crabapple's venison, the imagery of Coleridge, and the flight paths of our native birds.

The plum orchard belonging to Blankhill Farm is, despite its name, situated in a lush dale, and we all spoke our admiration for it to the farmer who met us at the gate, his ears reddening with pleasure and bashfulness. Even Miss de Bourgh condescended to give it her favourable opinion. I endeavoured as best I might to conceal my astonishment.

We were supplied with wicker baskets by the farmer's wife and daughter and entreated to step inside the house if we should feel the slightest fatigue. Dr Reid soon lagged behind, engrossed in enquiry into the present state of the farmer's son, who, I gathered, had taken a bad fall a se'nnight ago. They cannot afford his services, but I would not put it past him to have arranged this entire outing merely in order to offer them, as it were, on the sly.

As Mrs Jenkinson and her high-born charge gravitated towards the east of the orchard, I and Ailsa found ourselves preferring the sun-dappled south. The air was ripe and fresh, infused with the scent of the drupaceous fruit, the low-cut trees drooping under their burden, as we too began to droop under the weight of our baskets, our hands stained and sticky with juices, our complexions bright with exertion.

"This is Heaven!" cried Ailsa. "This is life as it should be, you and me and Nature's bounty— Could anything be more glorious?"

I concurred with her sentiment, though I could not hold back a comment about how Nature's bounty fell sadly short, in this case, of providing any convenient places to rest.

She laughed and took my hand, not minding its stickiness in the least as she led me to a soft mossy knoll on the south-west edge of the orchard, where she lay down her greatcoat and invited me to sit.

"You'll catch a cold, Miss Ailsa Reid!" I scolded, a warm glow spreading through me at the prospect of sitting so closely together, out there in the open, yet without a soul to bear witness, without a person to see, to keep us from—

She said nothing, simply gazed up at me, as she had in the carriage, and I lost myself in that gaze, Lizzy, completely. I sank down beside her. I took her in my arms, wrapping my own cloak about the both of us, on the pretext of her recent illness, that her cousin should never forgive me... We stared at each other and there was not the faintest spectre of surprise in her expression, only a tender longing, a longing which it was incumbent on me to fulfil.

"Ailsa," I sighed, and she opened her mouth a little, and no other words were needed—no words in the English language could express this strange fever, this derangement at the core of my being, the reflection of which I saw writ upon her features as I leaned towards her—as I put my trembling lips to hers.

Her arms linked around me. Her breath was infinitely sweet, infinitely intoxicating, and I felt it was the most natural thing in the world, the sole purpose of my humdrum existence up until that moment to kiss those lips, to melt in the embrace of those arms, even as my heart palpitated frightfully, as some part of me stood aghast, stunned into momentary submission. Ailsa pushed back my bonnet, cleaving to me in a way—

"May the Devil take him!"

She let go of me as suddenly as I had—as we had—and was straightening her habit, rosy and annoyed. In my befuddlement, I thought she meant my husband, but no; as I came to my senses, I, too, heard the faint call of Dr Reid, persistently advancing on our position, and, quite instinctively, I rose to my feet and fled.

In which direction I ran, for how long, or what I was thinking, I cannot say, only that I couldn't stand it; I could not look him in the eye, not after what I had done, a breath ago, and with his cousin! I tripped over a root. I scraped my knee, muddied my petticoats, and tears pricked my eyes as I clapped my hands over my mouth to prevent the howl of misery threatening to issue forth.

A murmur of voices took me off guard; I huddled beneath the low-hanging canopy of the tree where I lay, where fallen plums were eating into the stuff of my skirt. The voices were female, that much I could tell, and as they drew nearer, though I could not make out the words muttered betwixt them, I recognised the fine silk of Miss de Bourgh's gown, the black boot of Mrs Jenkinson, and I dithered whether to make my presence known to them in my ignominy, or whether I should take my chances of them not observing me where I was, half covered by leaves and earth. If they did notice me, I could perhaps feign a fainting spell, unpalatable as the notion was; but as I was thus employed in internal debate, Miss de Bourgh's silk rustled, Mrs Jenkinson's boot stopped sharp, and I heard the unmistakable sound of a slap, followed by a deep, guttural groan.

My outrage beggars description: to think, Lizzy! Miss Anne de Bourgh physically reprimanding— I could hardly credit my faculties, my reason, and yet I heard it, clear and loud as the church bell, ringing out to saints and sinners alike.

At last, they moved far enough away that I dared venture my escape, and I dashed back towards the safety of the farm and the carriages, to my old life, where I knew nothing, nothing at all of the monstrosity of Miss de Bourgh, or, for that matter, what it was like to hold and to kiss a creature—a lady—whom one truly, genuinely, with all one's heart and soul—

I was met by Ailsa and Dr Reid, carrying our abandoned harvest, alarmed, as well they might be, by my wild appearance, my limping trot, my mud-spattered clothes.

Dr Reid made a fuss while Ailsa hung back, her face bleak, her eyes unnervingly dark. I could not let it be thus. I sought her gaze and held it; I offered the ghost of a smile until she returned it.

When Mrs J. and Miss de Bourgh joined us a quarter of an hour later, I was stowed away in the carriage with Ailsa. Queerly, I bethought myself of the turn of phrase Ailsa had used at the beginning of our acquaintance, to describe her aspirations for our relationship: the best of friends. The best of friends, indeed.

Hunsford Parsonage
October, 1815

Dearest Eliza,

It is Thursday night, and in the morning my husband will be back. I cannot believe a fortnight has passed already. I cannot believe it is not a lifetime.

I had word from Pemberley this morning, with a fuller description of your darling Jane, and some sentences about little Fitz and his papa for good measure. You are quite consummately besotted, lost to the world, and I comprehend you, more than you will ever know. I feel distinguished that you would write to me at all, in the first throes of your new attachment. I have, of course, scrawled down a few lines to that effect, and added all my well-wishes, by return post. But now it is night, and I sit down to write the longer, fuller epistle, which you will not receive.

How deceitful we are, even to our friends, when it comes to our innermost workings. I have spared you the true machinations of my heart for so long, however, that it has become second nature to me. Besides, what I am about to set down is not fit for the eyes of genteel society. By rights, it should not be writ at all. But you, my simulated confidante, must bear it all. You must indulge me. You have no choice.

Where shall I start? I feel as were I an inept scientist, striving to fathom and describe the particulars of a microcosm. My mind twirls with imagery, reels under the pressure of poignant moments, of shades and piecework that must be added to form part of the whole. I cannot say what I am any more. I can't make sense of myself. All I know is that I burn, and if ever man or woman burnt like this before... How could it be sin? How could it be termed pollution when the ardent flame is thus pure? But I wax poetic. It is the influence of this collection of poetry by John Donne, which Ailsa lent me. It won't do.

Ever since she came to tea on that first day of Mr Collins's leaving, ever since our plum-picking excursion, and all that it entailed, Ailsa has been a fixture in this house. And I have welcomed it; I have yearned for her to come back the moment she has gone in the evenings. At first, it was like having you back with me, like having untroubled girlhood back again, with all its passionate friendship and effervescent fancies. We have sat at our sewing, chatting for hours. We have sustained ourselves on oceans of tea, mountains of bread and butter. We have forgotten to eat altogether. We have tended Henry's grave, and slowly, patiently, Ailsa has examined the knots of my sorrow, not necessarily with a mind to untangle them, but to acknowledge them, to see them for what they are. She has teased me and called me Lucas, brazenly, and I have basked in the balm of her presence, in the rich depths of her eyes.

How simple it has seemed. For two weeks I have forgotten about my husband, my domestic concerns, my duties and obligations. I have forgotten about Lady Catherine and my family at Meryton, and yes, in some ways, even about you. I have got up in the morning for Ailsa. I have lain in my bed at night, filled to the brim with her. I have lived and breathed only Ailsa.

But I can pretend to innocence no longer. For now, I am truly split open. Now I have truly, irrevocably, lost my heart, my soul, my virtue. But mostly my heart.

What could have brought this about? Oh, Lizzy, it was the rain. The blessed rain.

*

The night before this I was invited to dine at the doctor's. The man has seen less of his cousin, almost, than before she came to live with him; but he does not reproach me. He was all affability, all cheerfulness and good humour. I have never known him to be this animated in company before. But then, I have never really known him. It is evident that his cousin's presence has wrought this change in him, and once more, I flinched to think that the logical conclusion to this mutually beneficial affinity must be a lawful liaison. As I watched them together, cheering though the prospect of keeping Ailsa indefinitely at Hunsford was, I could not but feel a chill at my breast, a sickening of my stomach, as unbidden images of 'dear Tom' performing his conjugal duties—his husbandly rights—encroached upon my mind.

Oh, do not turn away from me in horror, my Lizzy! Even as I have sworn to give a faithful account of matters in these sequestered letters, I cannot but envision what you must think of me, if you could see my innermost tumult and depravity laid bare.

My bitter anxieties made me grow quiet and troubled. I was ashamed of myself, heartily so. Here were two persons whom I had become so dearly attached to, within the space of a month; how could I begrudge them this felicity, this security in station and life? You would not recognise your practical-minded Charlotte in this selfishly jealous creature.

I barely recognise myself.

For dessert we had a delectable cherry compote, which Lilly had obtained from a neighbour, trading it for some 'lucky heather' she had carried about her person when they left G__. She presented the dish with a flourish, letting us know it was passable, and bringing us to the understanding that next year she would procure us a better specimen of her own making, if that scrawny tree out back would but yield a handful of the harvest of which Master Reid's butler was so fond to boast.

All three of us laughed and assured her that, naturally, we should like hers the best. And with that, the thunder came.

It was as abrupt as these things always are. One moment, it had been a fine, if somewhat stale evening; the next, it was pouring down.

Dr Reid stood to look out of the window, his visage at once solemn and serious, suited to a man of his vocation.

"The sky is wholly overcast," he murmured, scarcely audible over the ferocious torrent of rain. "It looks to be a storm. We cannot expect it to let up for hours. Mrs Collins, if I had but a closed carriage to offer to take you back to the parsonage, all would be well. But, as you know, mine has no top; it won't do. I must insist that you stay the night. You will not mind sharing quarters with Ailsa? Notwithstanding your short acquaintance, I know you have become the fondest of friends. Do excuse my impertinence, Mrs Collins, but as your physician, I really must insist that you do not venture outside in the rain. There is a fever about, and—"

"Oh! Tom, enough of your grave face. Of course Mrs Collins shall stay. There is plenty of room in my bed, and though Lilly has been known to complain that I am a fussy sleeper, I am sure we will make do for one night! You will stay, Charlotte? Say you will! Or shall I be forced to let Tom carry on his sermon?"

My consternation must have been apparent, for Ailsa's heretofore sparkling eyes grew concerned as she beheld me. She made a little gesture of entreaty with her hand, and, as ever, I could not say no. How often have we not taken our rest together in childish embrace at Longbourn, Lizzy? Nothing could be more proper than for two girls, two women, to share a bed. But since our visit to the orchard—I could not but wonder if the feelings the suggestion engendered in me fell rightly within the realms of innocence. I have heard people speak of girlish infatuation, but I am a married woman. I am thirty years of age. What I feel for Ailsa—

"Mrs Collins, I—"

"Oh! Certainly...pardon me...I was only thinking... I should be honoured to accept your offer—nay, I must; I am merely struck dumb by your kindness and consideration for my well-being. Indeed, I am most obliged to your hospitality, Sir!"

Dr Reid inclined his head and bowed, and we passed the rest of the evening in happy conversation, reading aloud our favourite passages from the great poets, until the frequency of our involuntary interruptions to hide our yawns announced that the hour for retirement had come.

Thanking me again for agreeing to stay, Dr Reid wished us a good night, and admonished us not to keep ourselves awake for too long with idle chatter. Ailsa batted his arm, telling him not to be such a tease, and that we were not fourteen-year-old girls anymore.

He laughed and went on his way.

With him seemed to go my ability to draw breath. Ailsa threaded her arm through mine, leaned her head on my shoulder, and said quietly:

"Take me to bed, Lucas."

For a moment, I thought I would surely faint. Instead, I summoned up my fortitude, striving to find my way back to the steadfast, dependable Charlotte of yesteryears, and started on the flight of stairs.

She followed my lead beautifully, effortlessly—as if we had been a couple dancing. As if we had been a couple, all in all. Odd, irreconcilable ideas sprang into my mind: I wondered was this how it felt leading your betrothed to church, was this how it felt leading her to dinner parties, to assemblies, to your house, and up to her chambers at night? Did William—

But I could not allow myself to continue in that strain. The parsonage was far away, cut off from me by a curtain of rain. That life—the life which I had chosen—was not mine to inhabit at the present hour. I was invited, for the briefest time, to partake of an alternative. Would you have had me decline, Eliza? Charlotte Lucas, Mrs Collins, most certainly would. But I was simply Lucas, accompanying my darling to our shared bedchamber for the night, and I would not, I could not demur.

As we came up onto the landing, Ailsa pressed my arm, indicating a turn to the left. We approached an old wooden door with a brass key in it, and letting me past her into the room, Ailsa slipped the key out of the lock on the outside and quietly locked the door from within.

She came over to where I was standing awkwardly betwixt her writing desk and the bed, and put the key in my hand.

"I want you to be comfortable, Charly," she said in a low voice, head bent to the floor. "I am sorry if I made you uncomfortable, insisting that you should stay. I could not abide the thought of— But no, I must be frank with you."

She peeked up at me, and her lovely, storm-laden eyes (Have I told you the colour of her eyes? They are a cloudy grey, the exact tint of the overcast sky; a shade which I had not given a moment's attention to, which I might have professed to be indifferent, even, before Ailsa Reid came into my life)—her eyes were awash with unshed tears, making me want to draw her into my arms and kiss them away.

To kiss her as I had done, for but a moment, among the plum trees; an occurrence to which we had not referred verbally, but which seemed to have coloured every thought, every utterance, every gesture since, so that we were wound ever tighter into an inexorable knot.

She must have read something of this upon my face, for she broke into a small, tremulous smile and seemed to gather strength for her successive speech.

"I want there to be no artifice between us. I want you to know, before you share a bed with me tonight, that I have wanted to share my bed with you since first I knew you. I have wanted... If you wish, we shall sleep together like maidens. But that is not what I want."

It took me a moment to recollect myself, to compel my tongue into action. It was indecorous of me to insist on her putting the matter more plainly, but we had already strayed far beyond the realms of decorum; I needed to hear her say it. I needed her to repeat my own unspoken desire back to me, as though I might have mumbled it on the other side of a whispering gallery.

"What is it you want?"

"I want to know you as a husband knows his wife."

I could not say a word. I could not think. I could only nod my head, and I did.

She fell upon me, and as she embraced me, my lips were at last on her anew, and she quivered and sighed in my arms. It was everything, Eliza. It was not enough.

I broke off our entanglement, struggling to regain my breath. Her countenance was glowing from where I had kissed her, blooming under my touch. It was the purest enchantment. She had me possessed.

All pretence was dismissed; I could not dissimulate. She had opened the floodgates, and all that had been dammed up must needs break through. Moving around her, I began to unbutton her dress. Ailsa stood quite still, eyes closed, her chest rising and falling with irregularity. I pushed the muslin off her shoulders and let it fall to the floor. Her eyelids fluttered. I embraced her from behind and began to kiss the sweet, milky skin that I had exposed.

"Lucas," she exhaled, and my hands came up of their own, untying and unclasping her stays. I smoothed my hands in under the layers, my palms finding the outlines of her back and ribs. She was warm and supple, responsive to my slightest caress. A formidable angel. I pulled impatiently at her chemise.

She whirled around in my arms and planted small, shy kisses along my cheekbone, down across my jaw.

"You too, Charly," she murmured in between kisses. "You too."

It took me a moment to divine her meaning. As I did, I turned around and obliged her in letting her help me out of my gown and undergarments. She was swift and skilful, her fingers nimbly divesting me of my articles of clothing, reminding me of how she had let loose my hair in her lap, was it but a few weeks ago? As she stroked my stays down my front, I leant back against her. Her fingers caught on the riband holding my secret-most key.

"What's this?" she exclaimed, then caught herself, her hand covering the lovely rosebud of her mouth. "Pray forgive me, Lucas. I am too curious; it was ever a fault of mine."

I knew the embarrassment must be visible on my cheeks, but I smiled bravely, taking her hand from her mouth and supplanting it with my lips.

"It's the key to the hidden compartment of my escritoire," I replied at length. "I keep it with me always."

I made to take it off. She stayed my hands.

"Keep it," she whispered thickly and cleared her throat. "I should like for you to keep it on. What do you write about, that you must keep it under lock and key?"

"Thoughts—impressions, mostly," I said vaguely, blushing, wanting to hide myself from her meaningful gaze.

"Do you write about me?"

I met her eyes, and they were filled with such earnest solicitude, such tender yearning, I fairly melted before her feet.

"Yes," I admitted. "I do."

She wrapped me up in a passionate embrace and kissed and kissed me till we were both faint and out of breath.

Pressing her lips to my ear, she made me quake with a rapture I had never known before.

"Take me to bed, Lucas," she repeated. "Take me to bed and I shall give you something truly worth writing about."

A thrill of anticipation leapt through me. With bare-faced eagerness, I unlaced her underskirt, caressing it off her hips, until it lay in a heap about her feet. I let my own follow suit.

Ailsa lifted the many layers of counterpane, blankets and sheets on the bed, and slid underneath. She beckoned for me to join her, which I did, gladly, wantonly, without a trace of indecision, without a shred of the embarrassment which I seemed to have thrown off with the last piece of my habit.

Soft and warm and urgent, Ailsa clung to me and I gasped with the delightfulness of it, the reality of it. I was there, I was hers. Completely. There was nowhere and nothing else in the world I would rather be.

"I want to touch you, Charly. I want to know every part of you. I can never be content—"

Tears had sprung up afresh, streaming down that angelic face, and I took it between my hands and kissed it, rubbing them away with my thumbs.

"Touch me," I begged her. "Know me. Love me."

She inhaled fiercely and crushed herself to me, until finally her hands began to move, exploring every nook and cranny of my person, lighting fires of ardour wheresoever they went.

"How wonderful," she sang. "How enchanting. What a beautiful, dear, perfect creature you are."

I could not properly string my letters together, let alone words, sentences. As though the Pentecostal flame was upon me, in reverse, stripping me of language, I felt myself hum and sigh with nonsense sounds beneath her touch. Have you ever experienced such a transport of happiness, Lizzy?

I wish to God you have.

Panting and squirming, my being seemed to topple upon the point of some imminent crisis. Ailsa's hands roamed lower, stroking and outlining the tops of my thighs. I held her to me with all my might.

"Yes," she gasped. "Oh yes, my love, my sweet. You are so close."

And yet, even then, I did not know. How could I have known? All I knew was that I was consumed by this longing, this powerful, indescribable wish for her to do something, anything that might quench—

"Please," I managed. "Please."

She kissed me deeply.

And then her hand found its way to my most private parts, and she found me— Oh! But she found me, and she stroked and pulled and clasped and tickled, and she knew; she knew indeed, and she swallowed my outcries, my ecstasy unravelled with her kisses, and she pushed me, shaking and paroxysming, over the brink to Paradise, again and again and again.

Oh, the rain. The blessed, blessed rain.

I must break off, Lizzy. Indeed, I must.

*

Friday noon. William has come, punctual as ever. I was in the breakfast parlour, drinking my morning cup of hot cocoa, anxiously awaiting his return as the gig pulled up.

Anxiously awaiting his return? Yes. Although I now know that he is not, that he never can be a husband to me as D. is to you (and yet I cannot write his name properly— Oh! What is the matter with me?), he is in the eyes of the Law, of Men, of God (I shudder to think) my lord and master, my very life. My odious life. How could I have committed myself to such a man? I have not forgotten your protestations at the time, Eliza. But that love would be possible—love—for someone like myself—

Enough of my supererogatory whinings, as Miss Harlowe's 'loving' brother would have it. We beings trapped in Time and Place have an unfortunate tendency to learn from our mistakes but in retrospect. You see I have not entirely lost my wit. But as the wheels of Mr Collins's gig clattered over the uneven stone paving outside, as I heard the shrill tenor of his voice instructing the stable hand to unload his boxes &c., I could do nothing but quake and draw my hand over my face, repeatedly, as if I could rub away the culpability that must be stamped upon it.

Would he know? Would he be able to descry the unspeakable deed I have committed? To be cuckolded by a man— Oh! But by a woman!

For such I must call it. I will not allow myself to veil my sin by linguistic mincing about. I have been unfaithful. I would—I will—be unfaithful again, should the opportunity arise. The infidelity of my flesh is as nothing, of no consequence, compared to the waywardness of my heart and soul. Even at that very moment, waiting for the door to be opened, for Travis to inform me of his return, I could feel *her* breath upon me. I could taste *her* sweet kisses on my lips. I was blushing. I was torn by guilt. I was defiant. If he could not tell from the merest glance, then he must be a greater dunce than ever even your papa would have reckoned him.

Bursting through, "My dearest Charlotte," he greeted me, "how does her ladyship?"

He could not have absolved me more efficaciously had he entered the room suggesting Miss Ailsa Reid should take up residence with us.

I am uncharitable. Heaven knows what my rebelling mind will dream up next? Yesterday was Thursday; he would assume—indeed, I suspected glibly, looking over his harried traveller's appearance, his earnestly entreating mien, he would find my conduct of the night before last a graver offence because it had kept me from attending her ladyship's dinner party, than from any conceivable breach of my marital vows. Could this be so? Could this possibly—I knew the answer in my heart.

"Her ladyship did very well when...last I saw her."

"Come, my dear." And there was real anguish in his features, a foreboding creeping upon him that had nothing whatsoever to do with any imagined (or very real) extramarital activities on my part, and everything to do with my whereabouts, or rather my non-attendance yesterevening at Rosings Park. "Was she in good health when you left her last night? Naturally, you would not have imposed yourself upon her at this hour of the morning!"

"She was in excellent health, Sir, when I left her this Tuesday. Your arrival today, I am afraid, prevented me from having the pleasure—"

"This Tuesday! Mrs Collins!"

He sank onto the old yeoman's chair by the door—the one that I brought with me, whimsically, from the attic at the Lodge. It creaked considerably. We always did suspect the termites had got into it.

I could not keep my countenance. I had to pull my handkerchief from my pocket and improvise a sneezing fit.

"I am deeply disappointed in you, madam. My coming today, what does it signify? You must know my feelings—you must, indeed!"

He was overwhelmed, an overgrown boy close to weeping. Would my Henry have looked something like it, had he been suffered to live? A phantom pain passed through my soul. I extended my hand to my son and found my husband's shoulder.

"Do try to compose yourself, William. I cannot think that I have offended her ladyship. We had a storm on Wednesday. I was caught and obliged to pass the night in the village. On my tardy return, I sent word to Lady Catherine, begging her leave to postpone my visit until your arrival, so we might pay our respects to her as one. Her ladyship very graciously condescended to approve this postponement; indeed, Sir, her wish to see you as soon as possible upon your return from your journey has made her reschedule her habitual Thursday dinner party to tonight. I took it upon myself to vouch for your willingness to enter into this scheme. I hope I have not been amiss."

Such art, Lizzy! Such duplicity! And yet, I spoke only the truth, though the mind behind this brilliant surprise, so well calculated to divert my husband's attention from my own comings and goings, was not mine but Ailsa's. She had been the one who, after waking me with languorous caresses and shewing me, irrefutably, how fully I am under her thrall, had suggested, propped up against a pillow, cheeks still faintly aglow, how we might escape the tedium of Thursday night at Rosings and delight Mr Collins, all at once.

"I shall be sorry not to see you tonight" was my retort—petulant child!

"Oh! Lucas, I shall be sorry not to see you, too—indeed, I shall. But consider, after this night: how shall we see each other in company so soon and not give way to...? We must rein ourselves in. If I saw you tonight at Lady Catherine's, without her devoted cavalier to court her attentions away from us, from you, especially—I could not bear to have her reflect upon you tonight! I am afraid I might do something rash, something unpardonable. No— Let her have her ears full of Mr Collins. Let them entertain each other, so that I might have the peace of mind to sit quietly, feasting my eyes upon you. Do not deny me this simple pleasure, dearest, or I shall not be held responsible for what I do."

I took her in my arms. Simple pleasures, indeed. There is nothing simple in this. She was right about last night—yet I cannot but dread tonight, as much as I am impatient, all but wild to have her before me again. But on the arm of my husband, she accompanied by her worthy cousin—how can this ever be enough?

I have quite given up the idea that you would enter into my thinking on this, my imaginary Lizzy. Even your opinion is unsought after—I am beyond the pale. I am as much beyond salvation as your poor, misled sister. Could this all-consuming yearning be anything akin to what Lydia felt? But Ailsa is no Wickham; my heart shrinks from the comparison. If she seduced me, I needed but little inducement. Had she not... My mind balks to think...

My pulses pound too loudly for me to be intelligible. I will put you under lock and key now, my long-lost love. Á demain.

Hunsford Parsonage
October, 1815

Dearest Elizabeth,

Our visit to Rosings Park has passed by. How many times over the course of the last three years have I not had occasion to write that sentence? What a commonplace, what a repetitive mantra has not the name of that stately setting become in my correspondence—regular and invented alike? Yet today, I must own that visiting Rosings will never be quite the same again. I must mention this visit to you, to my mamma and to Maria, in my letters to come; but it is only here that I may indulge in giving a full account of all that took place. And indulge I must, while it is still fresh in my mind, on my lips, wanton creature as I have become. I will exorcise my abandon here, so that I might write to you all tranquilly, sedately, without causing alarm, giving you no hint that you are receiving a letter from anyone but dear, docile Charlotte Collins.

For Lucas, the evening passed as follows:

Lady Catherine had sent her carriage to fetch us, furnishing William with yet another reason to sing her praises—as though he needed it! From our interview in the morning up until my very toilette at night—he actually came in to speak to me as Travis was arranging my hair; but this is nothing out of the ordinary when he is excited; I have learnt to look upon it with equanimity—he was expounding upon her ladyship's inconceivable kindness, her extraordinary affability, her ever-gratifying condescension. His liking for me, I am sorry to say, seems to have increased tenfold on my 'happy thought' of introducing such a plan as this. My boldness—but of that he will not speak. All is well, for the present, in our poisoned Paradise.

I chose to wear my mauve frock, which has undergone a transformation from being associated with grief to being a banner of victory brandished on my first visit to Ailsa's (to the doctor's, I should say, but I am sick of interposing these superfluous men between us—even 'dear Tom'), braving any snide remarks which the fine ladies might chuse to make, and we arrived just in time, as William had fretted over an invisible stain on the inside fold of his cravat. He was all in a fluster. Poor silly, silly man.

Lady C.—as my clever love had foretold—was overjoyed to see him; a joy that manifested itself in chiding him most vehemently for letting the bishop persuade him into going off on this journey in the first place. Mr C. bowed low enough that I thought he would have fain fallen to the floor, grovelling at her feet like a puppy dog. I could not forbear a smile, though I felt a twinge of guilt at my gross caricaturing. I lifted my eyes from my stooping husband, and there, on the other side of him, as if he were bending over not to obstruct my view, was Ailsa.

I would have writ the Sun, for such was her immediate effect on me. I had a distinct impression of my skin, my limbs, even each strand of my hair, blossoming where her gaze touched upon it. Oh, but she was radiant.

How could I—how could anyone—look upon her and not want to hold her, not want to carry her off and... You see how it is with me. I wished, briefly, that I might have sought guidance in religion, but really. *Thou shalt not lie with mankind, as with womankind: it is an abomination.* (Lev. 18:22) I remember reading this passage during tedious hours of Bible studies and wondering, wondering. I still cannot say what it means. But I care not for repentance. The reputed keeper of my soul (that he should be also my husband, part and parcel!) stood up, and without thinking, I stepped a little to the side, that he might not spoil my view.

At dinner, the talk of Mr C.'s absence was eclipsed by Lady C.'s more pressing alarm at her daughter's growing indifference. Miss de Bourgh had not come down to join the party, I noted in a daze, and even Dr Reid conceded that she did not seem to be thriving at present.

For my part, I think the winter months depress her. She is a cross, unpleasant girl at the best of times, but in the winter she looks positively gloom-stricken. I have wondered that her mamma does not spot the pattern. Far be it from me, however, to have my nose boxed for butting in where my opinion is not called for.

Mrs Jenkinson, who is generally more quiet even than I am in this company, was twisting her hands, wetting her lips, and looking uncommonly vexed. I flinched as the sound of that slap, that awful slap amid the plum trees, echoed in my mind.

"Madam," she finally exclaimed, her voice risen to an octave that might have challenged the best sopranos. "Perhaps the doctor... This trip to Bath..."

Lady Catherine turned to Dr Reid, all but pointing at him with her knife.

"What have you to say, Doctor, on this scheme of ours of bringing Miss de Bourgh to Bath to take the water a month from now? Would not such a remedy do her a world of good?"

Tom put down his knife and fork, as if in surrender. What could he say, indeed, if her ladyship had made up her mind on the subject?

"I cannot see that it would have an adverse effect, if you ask my professional opinion, ma'am. Perhaps your daughter, though—"

"Very well, very well— There, Mrs Jenkinson, we must defer to the doctor's judgement. It is all settled. We shall travel to Bath in December, and you must all accompany us thither. I cannot abide either the physicians or the company of that town. I must have my own party. If you cannot afford the expense, you are welcome to share our lodgings at P__ Street. I shall not be pleased if you do not all come."

Her ladyship put her knife down on the plate before her, and the clang seemed to reverberate through the preternatural quiet that had settled over the dining-room. I glanced at Mrs J., and to my surprise, I caught a look of triumph in her eyes before she averted them, folding her hands demurely, quiescently in her lap.

Ailsa was the first to speak, the first to collect herself, but she was not looking at Lady Catherine; she looked directly at me, her pulse throbbing faintly at her neck.

"You are too generous, your ladyship. How will we ever repay your kindness? My cousin and I shall be delighted to join you."

On cue—which she must have known, sly creature—my husband broke into raptures, refusing to be outdone on such an occasion to shew his readiness to comply with anything the high-born lady might ask of him.

I will not repeat his speech. To be perfectly honest, I hardly attended to it. All my attention was rapt on Ailsa, a strange smile playing on her features as she took hold of her wineglass and had a sip.

She wanted us to go to Bath. But why? I could not make sense of this turn of events.

*

Shortly after dinner, the card tables were set up, but as Miss de Bourgh was not in company we were too few for two tables, and too many for one. I gave up my place to Mrs Jenkinson, whose thrill in the game all but equals her mistress's, and wandered off into the library—hoping, hoping.

Yes. As I was opening a musty tome of Hunsford memorabilia, two slender arms came about my waist, and I leant back, drinking in the warmth and presence and reality of her. Had it been but two days? Already, my mind had started to question itself so that I have had to resort to reading these incriminating pages, over and over, to convince myself that the incredible actually did take place.

"Someone might come," I sighed as I held her arms tighter around me, my body and my common sense at utter odds with one another.

"Lady Catherine is lost in her cards," Ailsa mumbled, her soft lips tickling my neck. "And there is no one about to stand in for any of the others. She would hardly allow a footman to sit down with her."

She placed little kisses down my neck, right along the edge of my gown, causing a faintness to come over me. I swayed, slightly, in her arms, and closed my eyes.

"I do love this frock on you," she continued, even as I could hear the swoosh and rustle of my wool and then my silk petticoat being lifted. I had put on my finest, on a whim, as if I had expected... She cupped her hand around me, through my linen, and I swallowed a moan.

"I want you." She breathed into my ear, her curves pressing insistently against my back, and I thought *You have me. You have me irredeemably.* But I could not speak.

She rubbed at me through the thin cotton of my drawers, and I blushed as I noticed how damp the stuff was. Ailsa could not but feel it, too, and she quivered against me, gasping into my hair.

"I must have you. I must have you completely."

All but this overarching need disappeared: the sepulchral library, the boisterous conversation of the card players but two doors down the hall, the possibility that some servant...

I could not stop myself. Whatever the consequences, I could not stop. I turned my head to receive her kiss, pushed against her caressing hand. She needed no further invitation. Swiftly, she slipped inside my underthings, and just as swiftly—for I was ready for her, prepared in a way I could not have dreamt a person could be ready for another—her fingers slid inside me, delving deep into my very centre.

I ached with passion. I thought I must surely swoon.

But my fair seductress would not let me off so easily, would not let me melt away without reaching that point of crisis, that pinnacle of pleasure to which she had so recently introduced me. She pulled me tighter to her, and as she continued to move inside me, her free hand came up to fondle my bosom through the layers of my attire, stroking and pulling until the tips were swollen buds, little nubs apparent through the material of my dress, and I would have blushed anew if my face had not already been oversaturated, if my whole self had not already been brimming, overflowing—

"Yes. Yes, do."

She pressed her lips fervently against my neck, and I clasped my hands over my mouth, muffling an outcry as that delicious eruption crested and coursed through me, blinding my vision momentarily, stiffening my limbs as if in shock.

Such is her power. I was undone.

Ailsa kissed me fondly as I came to, limp and spent in her arms, and she straightened out my gown, as best she could, while I steadied myself against the bookcase, struggling to regain my composure. Her eyes shone as she beheld me, her features, her entire décolletage tinged scarlet.

"You are the most charming creature I ever laid eyes on, Lucas. Would to God that you were mine."

I stared at her in bewilderment. I was mute, unpardonably, heinously mute. Her eyes glossed over, and she shook her head, smiling hollowly at my belatedly proffered embrace. Turning her adored self from me, she walked out of the room.

I should have run after her, falling at her feet, declaring myself—but I was too weak. I was too wary, to be truthful, and I must be that: the whole precariousness of our situation came crashing down upon me, rooting me in place.

I love her, Lizzy. I worship the very ground Miss Ailsa Reid sees fit to tread upon. But what can be done about it? What on Earth can be done?

Hunsford Parsonage
October, 1815

Dear Lizzy,

It has been two days since last I saw her. You cannot fail, by now, to know to whom I refer. In the meantime, I have received a letter from my sister, absolutely fixing the date of her arrival to Thursday morning, a week from hence. This means, of course, the poor girl will have but a few hours of repose before she must be included in our dinner invitation to Rosings (Mr Collins has already set about procuring her this honour), but we all have our crosses to bear. It struck me, besides, that Maria has never been much averse to waiting upon her ladyship, even if over-awed into dumb acquiescence by that lady's presence. She always liked grand places, fine things, the ostentation of the lesser nobility. Silly goose.

You can tell I am uncommonly irked. I cannot abide my husband's constant presence (and it is a year—a year!—until his next Canterbury peregrination), and I have little patience even with Travis. She bears my changeable temper with heroic fortitude, of course, which irks me further. I blame it on my headaches—which have, indeed, been frequent of late—but I can see from the way in which her eyes hang about my midsection that this is not the principal cause to which she attributes my ill humour. Well, she is mistaken. I had my monthly indisposition but two weeks ago—something, I dare say, with which she should be well acquainted, since she takes our laundry out. But there is another, more cogent reason I know it cannot be: I have not, after all, shared my bed with Mr C. since... Oh! Shortly before Miss Ailsa Reid arrived at Hunsford, if you must know. Do not remonstrate with me, Eliza. I know it must be done. I know if I do not go to him willingly, he will... My feelings are all inverted. What I should feel upon breaking my wedding vows, I feel instead, blackly, at the thought of fulfilling them.

I am not afraid of falling with child, however. After I lost Henry (and now I will shock you again; perhaps more so than ever), I was so distraught by the idea of bearing another child so soon after his passing, I could not eat, sleep or drink from the grief-mingled horror. I felt as though I was possessed of a murderous womb. I cannot explain it to you, sweet, maternal Eliza—I could not speak of it to anyone. But the nurse who attended me upon that fateful night... Suffice it to say that it turned out I was not unique, after all, in my unnatural emotions. She came to see me, but a week after, and shut herself up with me, in order to teach me to use a tincture of vinegar to prepare myself, as she said, for my husband's visits. She meant well, I am sure— Her object was merely that I should not overstrain my body for a few months yet. But the precaution proved so effective I have been using it ever since.

I cannot have another child. Most especially, I cannot now. I cannot.

I must interrupt this bad-tempered effusion and go to make preparations at church. I have promised William, and this, at least, is one promise I can keep. I will pick up my pen again this evening, if indeed there should be anything more to say. Oh, despondent wretch! I shall endeavour to regain my serenity. To church, then—

*

Night. I may indeed write night, for it is just past one o'clock, and Minerva's favourite is hooting her praises outside my window. I am scribbling by the light of a tallow candle—you must forgive my scrawls. I should be abed, sleeping the erratic sleep of the wicked. My heart is full. My head is throbbing. Pen or prayer seem my only recourse. I chuse the former, as my use of the latter would perchance have a touch of the blasphemous. Oh, if I had but the power!

But I must start, for my own sake as well as yours, from where I left off.

I went down to our little church in a state of dim dejection, ready to prostrate myself on the floor. I did no such thing, of course. When I came in I was glad to see that Mr Wilkinson, the caretaker, was not about. I exchanged my cloak for my apron there and began to wash and grease the pews, happy to escape into this piece of ardent manual labour. Are you ever permitted such relief at Pemberley, my dear? You have the rearing of your children, at least, which I know you will not have wrested from you, even at the price of being considered the eccentric mistress of low-born beginnings. Despite my own melancholy, I must own it was a beautiful autumn day without, and the golden sunlight fell in glittering cascades through Mr Wilkinson's newly washed windows. It was the most picturesque setting for a wholesome Sunday service. And the physician and his cousin would, in spite of everything, be sure to come.

Yes, Miss Ailsa Reid would be mine to gaze upon today. She would sit in this newly polished pew, where my hands had rubbed and stroked. She would be wearing her silver-grey bonnet, the one which brings out her stormy eyes, and the yellow light of the sun would fall through the stained glass to touch her white face and hands with a multitude of colour.

You think I was too particular in my fantasies, Lizzy? I confess, it would not be the first Sunday my eyes rested more on the lady in question than on my husband in his pulpit.

As I was standing there, lost in the splendour of my inner vision, my heart leapt to hear the door of the church being opened. The light steps and the susurrus of layers upon layers of cloth divulged the sex of the visitor, before she came into view.

As she espied me, her mouth formed a perfect, inaudible oh. She was indeed wearing her grey bonnet, her velvet cloak, offset by the sheer pink in her gloved hands. Another rose. A living, breathing Ailsa.

"I did not know you would be here," she said, her heart-shaped chin rising slightly. Her eyes still held the hurt of two nights ago as she looked upon me. I could not bear it. This might be my only opportunity, so propitiously given me I glanced warily, gratefully, at the altar. I threw myself on my knees before her, the cold stone floor jolting me, my arms stretched out in supplication. She looked aghast, stepping back as if I might burn her should I come too close.

"Please," I entreated her. "Please, do not be angry with me. Tell me what I have done."

She closed her eyes. I felt a vexation at my chest, as profound and as hopeless as when I realised... But hush. She opened her eyes anew and a profusion of tears wetted her cheeks, wetted me as she fell to meet me, as she fell into my open arms and kissed me violently, with a desperation that fairly matched my own.

"Oh, Lucas," she breathed into my mouth, and I clasped her to me, as though I might join us together, eternally, simply by fastening my arms around her. Join us in wedlock. I winced. My soul shook.

Her gloved hand came up to stroke my face, and I shivered at the softness and warmth of her, even through this second layer of skin. I blushed at myself. She rewarded me with a small smile, betwixt her tears.

"Do not be ashamed of your reactions to me, Charly. Never be ashamed of that."

"But..." I fell silent. How could I begin to explain the mess of my warring emotions, when I have not even been able to state them clearly here, in the privacy and seclusion of my own chambers, in the dead of night?

She swept her finger lingeringly along my jawbone. "Is there somewhere we might go?" It was her turn to blush, which she did, as all things she does, charmingly. "To speak."

Rakish Freke as I have become, I would not have minded if it were not to speak. I dipped my head, and in a sudden fit of needing to prove myself—needing to prove to myself that I, too, held some of this strange power over her—I pulled off the glove on her left hand and raised her bared fingers to my lips. She gave out a hiss of air.

Emboldened, I let the tip of my tongue slip between her ring and long fingers, finding the soft and slightly salty folds there. Her countenance was burning, a deep crimson that licked all the way down her neck and throat. My insides fluttered.

I stood and reached out my hand to her, which she grasped firmly, although she rose somewhat unsteadily. I will not hide my feelings from you: I was delighted. Exultory. I felt like the King of Kings. Together, we walked up the nave of the church, past the empty aisles, and turned off onto one of the wings just before the altar, leading unto the vestry. William would not be there yet, and neither Mr nor Mrs Wilkinson ever intrudes upon this part of the building. We had an hour. Maybe two.

As we stepped in, I locked the door to the main church hall and quickly crossed the room to check that the outside door was bolted. I tied off my apron and hung it on its peg. Ailsa stood irresolutely, hands folded across her chest, in the middle of the room.

"Lucas," she said, and I came up to her and kissed her. She met my lips willingly, greedily, yet she put her hands on my shoulders, very lightly holding me back. I circled my arms around her waist and drew her to me. The welcome heat of her all but turned my head.

How can I make you understand? A hopeless quest, perforce—but how can I make myself understand? Perhaps all I can say is that standing there, with this wonderfully desirable creature, this woman (I will write it) in my arms, half wrapped up in her cloak, her bosom pressed against mine, her bonnet slightly awry, I felt—at peace. At home. But more than at home: it was as if I had never truly known what home was until I found it, quite haphazardly, in the embrace of Miss Ailsa Reid. I would be her waiting-maid rather than Mr Collins's wife. Well, naturally. I would be her maid rather than the Queen of England!

She put her head on my shoulder, sinking into my embrace. The tenderness of it stirred me deeper even than the passion, which, I must own, was still raging within me.

"We cannot speak like this. How will you listen to what I have to say? How will I be able to speak at all, when I would a hundred times rather put my lips to better use?"

I took her meaning, but I was loath to let her go. I felt as though had my husband chosen that moment to walk in on us, I could not have let her go.

"I missed you," I said frankly. Her face crumpled and she began to weep in earnest. "No, Ailsa, this won't do." My own eyes were welling up as I let go of her to remove her bonnet and dab at her tears with my sleeve. "Pray forgive me, forgive me a thousand times—but tell me how I have offended you."

"Offended me!" The words burst from her with such force, I almost thought she would have slapped me.

My hands fell to my sides. She sat down on the wooden bench that skirts the western wall of the vestry, and I fell to my knees again, in front of her.

"For heaven's sake, Charlotte! Will you stop lowering yourself before me and sit by my side? Are we not equals? If anything, I should be the one who humbles myself before you. You are the married woman, after all."

Her words smarted like so many arrows finding my weakest spots and burrowing their heads in my flesh. She was Diana, the virgin goddess, Goddess of the Hunt. I looked up at her. Her expression softened. She beckoned for me to sit by her again, and I complied, hiding my face in my hands.

"Charly..." She put her hand on my shoulder. Her fingers trembled. It gave me strength.

"What would you have me say? What would you have me do? You must know, Ailsa—surely, you must."

She looked confused.

"What must I know?"

"That I—" She put her hand over my mouth. Once more, her eyes filmed over. Once more, my spirits sank.

"Wait," she spoke, her voice barely audible. "Do not say it. Let me speak first."

I felt as though she had pushed the declaration back down my throat, into my swelling chest. I would not have it thrown back at me. I took her hand from my mouth, and held it in my lap.

"I love you, Ailsa Reid. Nothing you say can change that. Now speak."

I could see the conflict playing out in her eyes. She was angry. She was glad. She was—chagrined?

"You make it impossible. How can I tell you about myself when you—how can I risk losing—Oh! Why, Lucas? Why did you have to—"

My patience was worn down. I was maddened, untethered, and yet I knew, instinctively, that she was not rejecting me. Brazenly, I pulled her back into my arms. She did not resist me. Instead, like a child, she bent her head to my bosom and bedewed it with her tears. I rocked her, and shushed, and could not forbear kissing the top of her head. She turned it, to let me kiss her face, which I did, and—

Oh! Lizzy, but she was lovely, perfect, and I was out of my wits! I cannot forgive myself. I kissed her deeper, crushing her to me, and she lay in my arms, giving herself over to me completely.

She had made me hers. Could I...?

I stroked along the fabric of her frock. Her cloak had fallen open, her skirt already twisted halfway up her thigh. I let my fingers play along the hem, half lifting it, finding the edge of her stocking, her garter, the sweet, supple skin of her exposed leg. The palm of my hand flattened against it, tingling. I delighted in the warmth of her, the closeness of her, the tips of my fingers itching to explore... She moaned into my mouth as I found her, at last, warm and soft and moist, so infinitely inviting, and I wish I could say that in that last moment, I recollected myself, I reconsidered; but even as the thought, unbidden, came into my head—*I am deflowering her. I am taking what is not mine to take*—she sighed anew, lifting herself towards me, and, God help me! The deed was done.

Was it shock and self-loathing, a keening angst rising within me at my unpardonable violation of this last boundary—the holiest, the most sacred, the undeniable privilege of he who would swear to protect her and hold her dear for all time to come—which pulled me up sharp, froze me in place, even as she encompassed me, even as I was caught, by myself and by the Almighty, ravishing the sweetest flower in His Garden?

No. Not even this excuse, paltry though it is, can I claim in my defence. A noise came from outside. There was the sound of the church door being opened. There were steps.

We stared at each other. Ailsa was in wild disarray, her features rosy, her clothes dishevelled, my hand... I shut my eyes, pulling myself out of her. She sat up, straightening her habiliment, finding her bonnet on the table where I had left it, carelessly thrown aside. I was numb and mute, at a loss—lost.

For the second time that day, she stroked my cheek, and as I finally made myself look into her eyes, expecting my doom, my condemnation—how could she but hate me?—I found them clear and bright, brimming not with tears but with sincere and earnest affection.

"It's best I go, Charly. You look culpable enough without me by your side. But please do not... Please think kindly of me, if you can."

I gawped. She kissed me lightly on the lips.

The steps had begun anew, after a pause, walking steadfastly down the nave, walking—there was no denying it now—directly towards the vestry.

"I must go," she repeated tenderly, the tone of her voice giving hope, unreasonably, where all hope of future felicity must needs have been lost.

The fierceness of my anguish must have shone through my weak verisimilitude of a smile.

"Oh! Lucas, what is the matter? Do I disgust you so?"

I stood up. The steps, the wretched steps!

"You could never disgust me," I whispered under my breath. "But I have ruined you. I can never..."

I could say no more. We had reached the outside door, just as the steps were come up to the churchward one.

Ailsa was shaking her head, her countenance stark with concern, but there was no time— She must out, and she made a sign, her right hand seeming to pinch something from the air, the outside air, for I was, even then, closing the door about her. I heard the scraping of a key, a lock being turned, and I whirled about, my back to the wall, guilt writ large, I doubted not, upon my face. William stepped into the vestry, a bemused expression upon him, carrying Ailsa's rumpled rosebud in his hand.

"My dear!" exclaimed he, and then, even he, my blind Master: "But you look poorly."

I could have wept or laughed with bitterness— anything would have been preferable, but the pink in his hand, the sharp monochrome of his attire, my bewildered, bleeding heart, the stabbing pain that erupted at my temple. In short, I wilted to the floor.

*

And there you have it. I was, of course, excused from church, smelling salts administered, Travis ushered in to attend me to my bedside. Even Mr Collins—for all his concern at Lady Catherine's disapprobation—would not have a fainting woman at his service.

As we came back to the parsonage, I insisted on having a note carried to Dr Reid's, on pretence of sending for some more of Miss Reid's miraculous herbs. I agonised over the phrasing, worried the note might be read by the butler, by Lilly, by Dr Reid himself, before reaching the eyes for which it was intended. Finally, through a haze of pain, I jotted down:

Unwell. <u>Please forgive me.</u> Pray send some of your herbal tea, if convenient. Your servant, C.C.

Within the hour, the stable hand came back with a parcel of herbs, and a short note to this effect:

Tom off to church. A fuller epistle will follow. Your much concerned, A.

A letter to follow, she wrote, all those hours ago. I am tense as a string, ready to either sing or burst. Did she change her mind? Did something happen to forestall her? I have been lying on the sofa in my chamber, where she had her hands in my hair, that time—where she first, as it were, undid me—drifting in and out of consciousness, in and out of pain. At some point in the afternoon, my husband returned from his offices, begging leave to attend me, but at my instruction, Travis firmly declined his entrance at the door.

It was not fairly done of me. Lizzy, what have I become? This cannot continue. Indeed, it cannot. What choice do I imagine myself to have? My choice was made, years and years ago, even before I gave myself away to a man whom you had rejected, because I could not have...

Another pang. It is past three. I must lie down.

Hunsford Parsonage
November, 1815

Dear Elizabeth,

It is morning, and I have had her letter. I see now how she must have been at her writing desk from the moment she returned to her cousin's, scarcely pausing to eat nor drink. I am excessively... Oh, I am overrun! But you shall have her letter enclosed, as though you could indeed advise me in so delicate a matter. I am relieved, selfishly so. I am grieved to the point of madness. I must go about my poultry. I must find some employment, or I am likely to wander around my rooms squalling until my husband breaks in upon me—and what good could I do, locked away in some dreadful asylum?

You would not judge her, Eliza. Your sisterly compassion must needs be awoken by this singular example of the mires and pitfalls of our unfortunate sex.

As for me, with my tenderer affection in this instance, with my <u>love</u>... I am worn out from weeping. I am incensed to the point of demanding blood for the blood that has been shed. I can taste its leaden flavour in my mouth—but I have bit my cheek, again and again, to steel myself through my second and third perusals.

I will go about my poultry. I will stop myself from wringing my hapless cock's neck.

Hunsford
3rd November, 1815

Lucas, my love—

I should not address you thus. But I have tried various ways of commencing this missive to you for three quarters of an hour, and it won't do to throw any more paper away. I must trust to your generosity. My feeling is pure, even if my mode of expressing it— but I cannot, I will not ask your pardon. Almost from the first night we met, I knew that I must adore you. Do you remember how valiant you were, love? Can you think that a heart like mine, so little used to the kindness you had to offer, would remain untouched? After a week I knew... And here you may justly blame me.

Do not imagine but that I blame myself, Charly. Starved as I was of human affection, hateful and spiteful, and seeing you, my darling, fettered to a man who could not be your equal if you should both live for an eternity—and yet, what gives me the right, if I should have been ever so taxed by Fate, to steal my succour from another's table?

But I care not for your Mr C. Forgive me, my dear, but I cannot. I know not by what method he came by you, that *you* should be his wife! It beggars belief. How can it be? What could have occasioned this flagrant mismatch on your side? How could your relations—but I shall stop myself, afresh.

I have no right to question you upon this point. You are what you are, a wedded woman—you are—I must write it, though my hand shrinks from the office—Mrs Collins, and my disingenuous device of styling you anything but will gain me nought but a self-destructive dream.

It is worse than that. If I were only giving pain to myself, if I were only throwing myself away, I would gladly damn my soul to the Eternal Fire, for but an hour in your arms.

But I have, wilfully, overlooked what it might do to you. I have been going around in a daze these last few weeks, and I find it painful, wretchedly so, to wake myself. The frenzied passion I have allowed to overtake me seemed but my due. What a self-serving, conceited creature my uncle's negligent malice has wrought. Even so, as you see, I cannot bring myself to ask you to give me up. Whichever way I turn, I see misery before and behind me. I thought, if I could but, with the assistance of my dear cousin, find a temporary shelter from my persecutions—

But how can I ask that you understand me, when I am presenting everything to you in this helter-skelter fashion? I must begin afresh, and from the start, truly, this time.

My dear Mrs Collins,

My name is Ailsa Marie Reid, and I was born a little more than twenty-one years ago. My parents were Sylvia and Patrick Reid, of G___. My mother was the last of an old line descended from Thun in

Switzerland, and my father was the youngest of three brothers, the oldest of whom you will have heard me and Tom refer to as our uncle and guardian, for reasons I will plainly lay before you, or as plainly as my vexed mind will allow.

I have few memories of my parents. A kind face, a warm caress—fragments of a bliss which seem as likely to be the inventions of a love-starved child as true recollections. But it is my dearest fantasy, my tenderest hope, to think that I was a contented babe. You will, I am sure (for I know your generous heart), understand why when I tell you that I was not four years of age when that horrendous calamity took place, which was to rob not only myself but also my favourite cousin of all the parents we had between us. On that fateful day, my parents and Tom's father were travelling together from Bath, in my uncle's chariot and four, when they were overtaken by highwaymen—a particularly sinister band—who left but the half bludgeoned driver alive to tell the story of what had befallen them. Thus, in one fell stroke, Tom and I, at eleven and four years of age, were left orphaned, at the mercy of our uncle G___.

My tears are diluting the ink, but do not pity me! I have pitied myself enough on this score; and perhaps, had I not, I would have been more sensible as to the repercussions. You will know from our fond reminisces that Tom and I were raised more or less as brother and sister on our uncle's estate. But what you may not remember, as it pains me even to mention it in casual conversation, is that my uncle in turn is not childless. Our cousin M___'s mother died in childbed. God rest her wearied soul, for I cannot think (I have not your generosity, Charlotte) that my uncle was ever an easy man to live with. M__ (forgive me for insisting upon this effacing of his name) grew up by our sides, although his by turns churlish and haughty temper caused Tom—who was his senior by but a few months, though infinitely his superior in intellect and feeling—to prefer the company of a childish girl rather than that of a backstabbing, irksome boy.

Thus far, I have led you to believe that our uncle was cruelty incarnate, but I must check myself. During our childhood, he was merely neglectful. Our cousin M__ had a private tutor, a kind-hearted man who took a liking to Tom's eager and peculiarly scientific bent of mind and proceeded to teach him on the sly, whenever his cousin found more amusing employment out of doors. I dare say this was not what my uncle paid the man for, and Tom keenly feels his debt to his old schoolmaster, a Mr Watts, whom he keeps up an affectionate correspondence with to this day, and whose pension he is pleased to contribute to, even if it has meant keeping his own household on a somewhat restricted budget.

For me, naturally, there was no formal instruction but our dear Lilly's, but my cousin Tom saw to it that I could read and write from a tender age. "You must write to me, Ailsa, when I go away. You must promise to keep me informed of all that happens to you," he used to say, with more prescience than a child is wont to have. We had the run of my uncle's library, and together with Tom, I developed a passion for learning and the natural sciences; though unlike him, I could not dream of going off to university. My uncle was loath to pay for Tom's studies, but when the time came and he was admitted on first application, there was little he could do to stop Tom from claiming his paternal inheritance, scant though it was. Yet through judicious investments and provisions that had kept it nearly intact from our uncle's avaricious onslaughts over the years, there was just enough to set Tom up for medical school.

My uncle G___ was furious. Indeed, you must not think I lay any blame at my cousin's door for leaving me behind. Tom, with his fondness for me, blames himself dreadfully—so dreadfully that I have not found it in myself to tell him all. There is not a soul in the world who knows all, but my sweet, loyal Lilly, and, if I can bring myself to finish this narrative, you, Charlotte. Yet to think—

*

I am back at my writing desk. Tom has returned from church, and persuaded me, against my inclination (for I must write before I lose my nerve) to take tea with him in the parlour. He knows fine well that there is not the slightest thing the matter with me, physically speaking. But he suspects; he is quick-witted enough. My dear brother—for so I term him between ourselves—has ever been acquainted with the curious nature of my heart.

We drank our tea, and ate our bread and butter which Lilly craftily provided. Tom informed me that

Mr Collins's sermon had been indifferent, that Mrs Collins was not to be seen (here he glanced at me), and that Lady Catherine had particularly complained to him afterwards that young ladies these days saw fit to beg off their religious duties for nought but a sneeze or a fainting fit. She did not speak too pointedly, however, as Miss de Bourgh and Mrs Jenkinson had likewise failed to make an appearance.

I told him of your hemicrania, and he was much concerned. Your standing with Tom predates my arrival here, dear heart, as well it might. I would have wondered at him, had I found that he held no particular regard for you.

But I am veering away from the point at which I had arrived before this interruption.

My uncle was furious. Greed might well be his overarching vice, commingled with the need to exert his influence over the people in his immediate surroundings—not, come to think of it, unlike our Lady C. What a pair they would make! But I jest only to deflect the main thread of my story, and you may find it in bad taste, darling Lucas, once we arrive at the point of crisis.

I was to call you Mrs Collins. It would seem my mind is too sprightly for penance, even when my pen is dipped in gravity.

As Tom slipped out of our uncle's reach, his hold on his remaining orphan tightened. What did he want with me? Why did he not throw me off, destitute, to fend my way as I would in the world, you ask, hinting—as indeed it might seem to the outside eye—

that there must yet be some familial attachment that bound him to me.

There was. It is spelled money, and they are left to me on the maternal line.

I was not to know, of course. But I blush to admit that Tom and I had, previous to his going away, ransacked my uncle's papers and found something to this effect. Upon further inquiry at Edinburgh, Tom managed to unearth my parents' solicitor and found that my mother's estate at St S___ in Switzerland was left, in its entirety, to her only child. I would come into my inheritance at the age of twenty-one, or if I were married before that time, the inheritance would fall to my husband.

Oh! Charlotte, this bequest is both the key to my liberty and the cause of my ruin! Without it, I cannot think but that my uncle should have had me sent away, married off—Lord knows what might have been my lot. Yet with it, his designs on me became, each day, clearer and clearer. I was destined for my cousin M___. I admit that the realisation filled me with revulsion.

—I must stop awhile.

*

There, I am steadier now. Lilly has brought me a glass of water. Unlike Tom, she is convinced that my feverish appearance is the sign of a return of my previous weakness, and she would fain take my pen and ink away and hustle me into bed. I do feel enervated. But stopping now will avail me of nothing but a respite, at the expense, I doubt not, of your further suspense.

Not for the world would I have you suffer on my behalf. Yet, if you do love me... My heart palpitates, swaying my resolve hither and thither. Know then, dearest one, that the misery I am about to unveil to you, though it must cause you fresh pain (this makes me twofold miserable) is now but an historical wound with me, which may not heal, truthfully, without leaving some scarification; but it is healing, thanks, in no small part, to you.

Oh, love, even this admission places you under an obligation that I would rather you were not compelled by. I want your affection, not your pity. But for you to give me the former, blindfolded, as it were—why, it is impossible, unthinkable. I would not have you give your heart to a chimaera. I must lay everything before you, regardless of how severe your judgement may be.

In spite of my growing awareness of my uncle's plans for me, I was certain, as I assured Tom in my letters to him, that I was safe from any advancements as long as I remained at his house, my twenty-first birthday being a few years away yet at the time. Furthermore, as I wrote then, my uncle did not suspect that I had any notion of there being anything left me on my mother's side. His usurpation of my paternal claims had, after all, been strictly within the bounds of the law of our kingdoms, and he was pleased to inform me, every se'ennight or so, that I remained under his protection by the goodness (indeed!) of his fraternal heart.

My cousin M___ took little to no notice of me during these years, for which I am, truly, very grateful. I spent my days in the company of Lilly, helping her with little chores, improving my sewing, or reading books from my uncle's library. I had no formal education in music or languages, which I longed for; particularly, as you may surmise, in the German tongue, as being the native language of my deceased mother. How I craved the schooling that my cousin M___ had squandered! He would not go off to university; an indolence my uncle, for his own nefarious purposes, was only too happy to indulge. Perchance he thought that Nature would take its course with two young people continually residing under the same forbidding roof? I know not. All I know is that the proximity, without the strong shield which Tom's presence had afforded, had rather the opposite effect. Every day, every hour, my cousin grew more repugnant to me. I confess, I have never been inclined to think well of the sex; even had my dear Tom made any advances of the sort, shewn any signs of more than brotherly affection, I would, as tenderly as I could have, put him off. I cannot say that I knew that I preferred women—indeed, there were none to prefer—but I knew that the words of John Donne resonated deeply with me, in that queer address penned by him of Sappho to Philaenis:

> *My two lips, eyes, thighs, differ from thy two*
> *But so, as thine from one another do,*
> *And, O, no more; the likeness being such,*
> *Why should they not alike in all parts touch?*

Oh! How I have longed to quote this to you! How perfectly this strangely gifted man, over a century ago, summed up my innermost workings. But once more, I am prevaricating.

Notwithstanding Tom's and my own apprehensions, it was not until a year ago that my uncle began to press the matter in earnest. I was coming of age, and it was becoming abundantly clear, even to him, that his son and I were not on an intimate, nor even a cordial footing. My cousin, somewhat to his father's dismay, had, contrariwise, begun to generate reproaches and whispered reports of his violent and unmanly conduct towards some of the unfortunate daughters of the local farmers.

I could not imagine—but now, I know too well what these reports tended to. How innocently, how foolishly I thought that I had but to plead my case with my uncle, reveal my foreknowledge of my waiting independence, and all would be well. If he cast me out—so much the better. I knew I could depend on Tom to offer me a sanctuary until such time as I should come into my own.

Had I forgotten my uncle's implacable fury at Tom's leaving?

I had not. I foresaw that he would be intractable. I expected to be prevailed upon, to be the recipient of his unbridled rage, even—yes, to be confined to my apartment. When I begged leave to go to my cousin Reid so as to impose upon my uncle's hospitality no longer, a terrible face came upon him, like unto a mask of war, and he swore savagely that he would rather I became the whore of the village poorhouse than that conniving devil's wife.

I was stunned into silence. My uncle had ever been a harsh, peevish guardian, but yet he had let me be brought up to think of myself as a gentleman's daughter, and I was utterly unaccustomed to such language from him.

What I had not expected, as I could not conceive of it—ignorant, headstrong girl that I was—was that my gaoler would not be my uncle himself, but his vile, unnatural progeny. What better way to coerce me into a solemnisation of such an alliance, after all, than to allow my cousin all the *rights* of a husband, until such time as I would be ready to beg for that which I would not consent to, when first proposed? What legal recourse could I have? I would be indelibly tainted in the eyes of the world, even should I proceed to present my case to public scrutiny. Alas. How simply are we thwarted. How easily are we plucked.

*

Oh! Charlotte, I have writ it. What must you feel on reading this? If only I could scrub myself clean and pure, as doves and lilies, as snowy pastures, and all those similes the poets are wont to employ; but the stain is forever upon me, although the sin, I contest, is not mine to bear. As I vowed to myself then, and as I must repeat, each morning, ever since: I refuse to be the tragic heroine of a Shakespearean romance. I will not commit a double offence upon my soul by letting my spirit be crushed by those who pretend to control my hapless limbs. I shall live. Lord help me, but I shall.

We have but this one life given us, my love. I will not apologise—

But there is more to tell, and the night is dark upon us. You are abed now, up at the parsonage, and I hope, I pray, that you may sleep.

You must promise me this, come what may, Lucas. Never again say that your love has polluted me. I know pollution. I have been fairly steeped in it. Your sweetness, on the other hand, is like a revivifying balm on my old, invisible bruises. Your touch renews me, like the fire devastates the forest, to let it grow back, young and green and full of life.

There was but one light in the darkness that encompassed me, and that was our Lilly, whom my uncle had neglected to banish from my side. Lilly was the one who cared for and nursed me through my humiliation, who swore that her master would be Master of her no more, and who proceeded, in her stalwart and imperturbable way, to plan our escape.

It would be impossible, we both knew, to hire a carriage, to trust any outsiders so close to our house to come to our aid. My uncle's estate is remote, and the nearby village and farms are all under his command, as completely as if he were, indeed, next to God.

We knew Tom would help us, yet we dared not endanger him by applying to him while we remained confined at G___. No, as I told Lilly, and to which she reluctantly agreed, there was but one recourse, and that was to make our flight across the moors, at night, and preferably through the rain, so it would be as difficult as possible for my uncle's hounds to pick up our scent in the morning.

I knew that they would not pursue us across the border, if we could but reach it. As imperious as my uncle is, as scheming and as criminal, he knew as well as I did that he had not the Law on his side. I had just turned twenty-one. And I was unmarried, if but nominally.

Lilly took care of everything, and you will understand now, dearest, why she is so patently indispensable to me. I know not how to begin to repay her for her services to me—forsooth, for risking her life for me!—yet she will hear of no remuneration, insisting, bleakly, that I carried the larger load. What she is referring to is merely that I had to endure those nightly visits, week after week, until we had all that we needed to take flight.

I did endure. My stomach roils to think of it, but I did endure.

Pollution! Oh, love! Never!

I will not harp on about it. I have writ enough to make your eyes bleed. Yet I must trespass upon your patience a little longer, for I have sworn that you shall know all.

It was a dreary and lowering day, the day we decided that we were as ready as we could hope to be, and that the weather promised the inclemency that would be opportune for us to make our way into the unknown. I was in a frail state—it could not be pretended otherwise—but I would not be dissuaded. To tarry would only have weakened me further. And, as I now know, it would have made escape unthinkable.

Oh! Charly, may God forgive me! To be fettered to that unspeakable place, to those unspeakable tyrants, for life!

But I did not know. To brood, to self-castigate, would that not, after all, be an ingratitude? I asked but for the opportunity to lead a life of my own making, to be the mistress, if not of my own estate (I dared not hope, indeed, that I would be able to obtain it), then at least of my own flesh and limbs. Perhaps you will think that this is a perversity, a disgrace to our sex. I will not ask you not to judge me, if you find my actions incompatible with the grain of your heart. I paid a terrible price. My breast heaves, my soul revolts at telling you. I remember your candid look, the openness of your features as you took my hand in the vestry and professed...

I will treasure it always. But I have not made the sacrifices I have made; I have not forsworn the world of men to live with the doubt that this love would not stand the test of knowing me completely. I would rather—though my hand quavers to write so, though it feels like, tastes like, blasphemy—I would rather you love me not than that you should love a mirage. I cannot be the ingénue you seem to have taken me for. I cannot be the paragon of womanly virtues. I am neither chaste nor humble. I am selfish, and wretched, and broken. I am not deserving of your or anyone's good opinion. By the conventions of the society in which we live, I am beyond salvation.

I cannot excuse myself. I do not regret it. I have acted, always, according to my own moral principles, rather than custom.

But I do regret inadvertently hurting others. You, Charlotte, and—

I must finish my history and be done with it. Enough of this pleading and mincing about. I will not insult your intelligence with these errant manipulations. You must form your own opinion; indeed, I would have you do so.

Lilly contrived to make herself housemaid for that day; the servants' duties in my uncle's household are carried out at their own discretion, as long as the work is done. There was, therefore, no suspicion of anything untoward, and her motive was simply to make sure that the gentlemen took their claret—as is their wont. Most importantly, we had to make certain that my primary gaoler would be temporarily incapacitated from carrying out his habitual office. If he came upon us leaving, all would be lost.

To this end, I had an ounce of a mild sedative Tom had sent me a few years before, while he was still at university, to be taken for a bout of night terrors.

Night terrors! You understand, I doubt not, that I do not keep the full extent of our relations' infamy from Tom to protect myself or them, but to protect him. Even if I could dissuade him from seeking vengeance, the pain his own impotence would cause him would cast a permanent shadow across his existence. He knows enough already; I must not make him desperate. My own burden would not be lightened by unnecessarily increasing the load upon his heart.

Incredibly, everything passed according to plan. Lilly left the masters of that gloomy house drowsing like cherubs upon the library chairs and let on to the butler that the rest of the household might expect a very quiet night. A stroke of genius—but you know, by now, that she is a very canny and resourceful creature. She hastened to my chambers and unlocked the door with the spare key which she—of all people!—had been entrusted with.

"Oh! Lilly, they will have you hanged if they should come upon us!"

"Nonsense, my lass," she chided me while helping me into my cloak, for it was, as we had wished for, pouring down outside. "Letting a young lady out of her chambers is no hanging offence. We are not serfs! And as for the drink, why, I doubt anyone will be the wiser. 'Twould not be the first time these fine gentlemen fell under the sleeping spell of their liquor."

"If anything should happen to you..."

She put her beloved hand to my cheek, and her eyes brimmed with such maternal affection that I fell silent, unable to express the enormity of my debt to her.

"We must make haste," she said gruffly. I took her hand, and off we went.

*

I will not bore you with the details of our flight across the moors. Even suffering, when it becomes repetitive, dulls our senses, so that which should at first pang be felt acutely becomes blunt and hardly worth the effort of recollection. You will be protesting, kind heart, but there is barely anything of those days and weeks that have made a lasting impression on me but that one morning, which shall be emblazoned upon my mind for as long as I draw breath.

We walked until our feet bled, our limbs swelled, our eyes were run dry of tears. We rationed the meagre store of food we had dared to carry with us to the brink of starvation. We slept fitfully, continually on the lookout for our pursuers.

I cannot say if we were pursued. Perhaps, after the first few days, they left us for dead upon the moors. Our untimely demise, after all, would not be at odds with my uncle's intentions.

I grew gaunt and spare—my devoted Lilly hollow-eyed and wretched. When the fever set in, I blush to admit that I welcomed it: the delirium that broke the humdrum of that never-ending landscape, the strange heat it afforded, the seductive promise of an end to our, as I felt then, futile journey. And yet we could not stop to rest. For Lilly's sake, if for nothing else, I could not give in to the temptation.

One morning, weeks after we had first set out, I woke up to a strange, keening wail. At first, I could not say whether it was from man or animal until I saw her: Lilly, huddled over me, her whole steadfast self shaking, her hands clasped in desperate prayer.

"Oh, Miss Ailsa, Miss Ailsa," she moaned in a terrible, broken tremor. "'Twas a bairn, Miss Ailsa. May God have mercy upon us!"

I tried to sit up to look for this unknown child, which had caused her such alarm. But there was a lassitude in my limbs, a paralysing weakness that seemed to shackle me to the ground. I lifted my hand to comfort her hysterics and saw that there was blood on it.

The child has butchered me, I remember thinking, before all recollection left me.

The rest of that day you must have second-hand, for I cannot piece it together for myself. Lilly has told me that I fainted away, and that she wound me in rags of cloth (her old petticoat sacrificed to this cause) to stop the haemorrhage and covered me with both our cloaks, more to keep me from being espied than to preserve me from the cold, as she says; for I was burning up. Through sheer force of desperation—I dare not presume to call it divine grace—she struck on a south-easterly direction and came, after but a mile or two, upon a scattering of cottages that make up the village of F___. I know not what history she gave us, but by aid of our small store of guineas she obtained help to carry me back to an old midwife who lived on the outskirts of this poor, forlorn place, and who was the closest thing to medical attention that the village of F___ afforded. And indeed, I have this kindly soul to thank for my life, for, as it happened, her skills in this particular complaint far outdid, I will wager, any well-studied medical man's.

As you will have concluded by now, my clever Charly, I had been attacked only by the unwitting child of my own womb. The small scrap of him (or her) had been buried in a shallow hole in the ground by Lilly, just before she left me, out of fear that any help she found would recant and leave me to die from my sin, if they came upon it.

There it lies, unmarked and returned to its maker, out on the forbidding moor. I have unearthed it only for you. I cannot say that I know what it is like to lose a child which you have hoped and prayed for. Do not compare your loss to mine. What kind of life would I have been able to offer this poor creature? It may be to compound and seal my guilt, but I cannot regret...

Enough. I have given you a faithful account of all. The rest you know, more or less. As soon as I was well enough to put pen to paper, I sent word to Tom that we meant to throw ourselves upon his good will, and we departed by post for Kent but a fortnight later, serendipitously supplied with a chest of garments that had been sewn up for me by the village seamstress, and which we paid for with IOUs, to be redeemed as soon as we had reached our destination. We dared not tarry, for fear that anyone might recognise us and give notice to my uncle. The village of F__ is far to the south of my uncle's estate, and neither of us had ever been there before; but it was upon Scottish soil, and I could not but feel, still within the reach of those wretches' grasping clutches.

Haply, I had, by some miracle, escaped any lasting infection. Only our Maker knows why He spared me, but I have interpreted it, wilfully, as a second chance to live a life of my own making, of devotion only to that which I hold truly sacred, which is, among other things, to be the servant only of those who are deserving thereof, to be

Your servant, madam,

Ailsa Reid

Hunsford Parsonage
November, 1815

Dear Lizzy,

It has been little more than a day since last I wrote, and yet it feels as if the universe should have turned during that time. I have seen her.

It is Tuesday night, and I have seen her, though it were for but one quarter of an hour that I could contrive to have some business at the doctor's. As you know (but now I am mixing the Lizzy of my imagination with the real Elizabeth Darcy—it is to her I have hinted at Mr C.'s continual problems of this sort)—as you, the other you, know then, I usually spend an hour or so of the afternoon on Tuesdays ridding my husband of lice. I could not think how to get out of this office, which vexed me, for more and more any intimate contact between us, even of the most trivial, innocent species, makes my insides churn, my skin itch to be washed. Scold me, indeed—I scold myself, but to little effect. I should—

But silence. Do not think that your Charlotte knows not what she ought to do, what it is her duty, to her husband, to her family, to her friends, to the world—in short, to everyone but herself, to do. Not to herself, Lizzy. If my darling's terrible history (and yet, her <u>bravery</u>) has taught me anything, it is that. *This one life.*

*

I thought there was someone at the door. Well, the someone who has a legal right to be at my door at this hour, for I have given him that right, in exchange for the mean comforts of a respectable life. I have contractual obligations. How bitter the taste of those words in my mouth. And how skittish I am, like a villain who knows he is about to commit a crime.

But where was I? The lice. I knew that I could not invite *her* to drink tea with us, for having her before me for the first time after reading her letter with *him* by my side—abominable, unthinkable. I could not write; my thoughts were too tumultuous to be put to paper; I feared, indeed, that if I started to write a response I should never have done with it! But to keep her in suspense, and then Maria coming on Thursday morning—no, I must see her, and—were my foremost thoughts as I came to in the morning, the pulse that was at my throat as I sat through breakfast, as I tried to focus my mind on Mr C.'s chatter, on my correspondence, on Travis's plans to obtain some clotted cream from the widow Hartley for Maria's benefit. Travis loves my sister dearly. This morning, it made me look at her, and think: if only...

But Maria shall marry for love. It was the one thing I promised myself, the one thing that might still make my marriage meaningful in any way. For her to marry for love—or not at all.

"Miss Reid promised me some lice powder."

William stopped himself mid-sentence, as well he might, for we were not speaking of anything remotely connected to either Ailsa or lice.

"I need it for later. And I need some air; I have been cooped up for too long. I shall take a walk into the village and call at Dr Reid's to fetch it."

"My dear—"

I looked upon my hands. I could not countenance—Oh! Eliza, I must take care.

Off I went as soon as ever I could get away, and I knew that perhaps I should have sent word, but I feared that she would take it upon herself to send me the lice powder, and that would not do. There was something despondent, something utterly disconsolate about the way she had closed her narrative. As if she was giving me up. Wise woman, you might say. I could not allow it.

At the doctor's, James led me into the little parlour with its queer collection of knick-knacks, which, over the course of but two months, has become so infinitely dear to me. I sat, wringing my hands, removing my gloves and putting them back on again. The door made its by now familiar creaking sound, and I stood—my heart beating so that I could barely keep steady, and there—there she was before me.

She was wan, tired-looking, but more beautiful to me, Lizzy, in that moment, than anything else upon Earth.

"Ailsa..." came over my lips, my feet of their own accord moving towards her.

"Mrs Co—"

I shook my head. I took her in my arms. I kissed her.

It was not an innocent kiss between girls, yet it was not like those passionate encounters that had fairly obliterated us on previous occasions either. I kissed her rather as though my life depended upon it, as though there was nothing else to say, nothing else to do—as if I could take all her anguish, her pain and regrets, and physically wrench them from her soul by way of her lips. I kissed her. I put my trembling hands, one gloved, the other exposed, to her muslin gown, touching her lightly through the layers of her habit, merely to ascertain that she was indeed there, all intact, as though my frenzied reading of her story had somehow put her through the maelstrom once more.

A sigh escaped her, even as her fingers undid the bow of my bonnet. She removed it, holding it in her left hand, as her right arm came up about my neck and pulled me closer to her.

"Lucas," she breathed against my lips. "Oh, Lucas, can it be?" and I felt as though I had been christened anew by her tears on my skin, by her soft arm around my neck.

I was Lucas in that moment. Lucas from here on.

The door creaked behind us. We leapt apart.

"Miss Ailsa, Master Reid wants to know..."

Lilly fell silent as she took in the scene before her, my tousled appearance—my wild eyes, no doubt—the dampness of her mistress's eyelashes, my bonnet still in her hand. Lilly put her hand to her heart, an expression on her face akin to that which she might have worn had she walked in on a rat feasting in the larder. A rat feasting on her most prized leg of lamb.

"Bless me," she muttered, under her breath.

Ailsa cleared her throat.

"What is it, Lilly? What does Tom want to know?"

Lilly seemed to recollect herself, though her eyes, I noted, were fastened on her mistress's forehead. She did not look at me.

"Master Reid wants to know if our visitor will be staying for tea, Ma'am. He just came in and would have come through himself, only he had some urgent papers to attend to. There's a letter for you, Miss, if I am not mistaken."

I cannot accurately put into words the change in the maidservant's tone of voice, in her stance towards me; there was nothing untoward in her speech, such as it was, yet even Ailsa was taken aback, her cheeks glowing, bursting out: "Lilly!"

"I will not be staying," I interrupted, as quickly as I could, for I would not have her quarrel with the worthy woman on any account, least of all mine, when truly— I turned to Ailsa, and upon beholding her, I could not but smile, a warmth spreading through my entire being. She smiled back at me. Lilly shuffled her feet impatiently, and thank God she did, Lizzy, or I know not what I would have done! I am bewitched. But that is an ugly word. I am— most heartily, helplessly—in love.

"I came to borrow some lice powder," I blurted, hoping that Ailsa would not be too confused, for I had not had time to explain my professed mission to her. I had not really had time to explain anything. But I hoped, as I kept my gaze steadily upon her, as I laid bare my soul in my eyes, that she knew all I could not say.

She lowered her head, still smiling, and gave me back my bonnet.

"Lilly, will you…" She turned to the maid, who was looking less than hospitable. "Oh, never mind, I will fetch it myself. Will you tell your master we shall not have the pleasure of Mrs Collins's company for tea? And do wipe that sullen look off your face. I was crying from a surfeit of happiness, that's all." She shot me a sideways glance. "I am very, very well."

Lilly lifted her eyes then, and the look she gave me was so full of distrust, such an inversion of every sentiment that I felt myself at that moment, it chilled me to the marrow of my bones.

She gave her mistress a curt nod, curtseyed, and followed her out of the room.

*

So that now, as ever, my happiness is mingled with fear. I wish I could ask your advice in earnest, my Lizzy. I wish I could escape this prison cell of silence and dissimulation.

For what she has done, for her heroism, we must verily term it, Lilly is deserving of nothing but the utmost veneration. Her apprehension—if that is what it is—that I would spoil her mistress's dearly bought and perilous equilibrium is not, I must fain admit, unfounded. But that look, that look of all-consuming disgust! I tremble at the by no means unjust accusation of it. For is she not right? Would not you and all the world join in her judgement upon me?

Oh! Ailsa, Ailsa, what have we done? What are we doing? And yet, how can I give it up? You are like the breath of life in me. You have animated me like the Sun animates the life force of the flower in springtime, which all through winter lay wrapped in waiting—and then.

Is it possible that Lilly suspects—?

I shall sleep.

Hunsford Parsonage
November, 1815

Dearest Elizabeth,

My sister is come, and it is a delight, I confess, to see her. How handsome she has grown; but then she always promised to become the beauty of the Lucases, if beauty there would be. You would laugh and say, playfully, that this is how one is apt to feel about one's favourite sister. That may be so, but give me leave to say that <u>your</u> favourite sister would indeed be considered a beauty by anyone's standards, and so you must give me, if you will allow me to have a scrap of sense and discernment left, the benefit of a doubt.

I will correct myself accordingly and say that Maria has still more of girlish prettiness than handsomeness, and that her eager obligingness further convinces one that she is, that she must be, a very pleasant thing to look upon. I think that I may call as my witness an, up until now, quite impartial judge on this score, but more of that anon.

I spent all of Wednesday in preparing for her arrival, for the little room at the top, with the pretty view to the trees that stand by the lane dividing us from Rosings, has been in disuse for too long. It reminded me of how much time has passed since last you were here, and then, of course, as a wedded woman, you stayed at your aunt's by marriage. It gives me pause, sometimes, to think that I will never again have the pleasure of accommodating you under my roof.

But here is Maria—I shall pick up my pen tonight.

*

We are back from the Park, after our second visit there since my sister arrived. Maria is very gay and sprightly and not so much in awe of her ladyship as has been her wont. That is to say, she still finds it almost impossible to put two sentences together in Lady Catherine's presence, but she has developed what might be called an effervescent charm in her reticence. Ailsa seems very pleased with her, which would make me love her even better, if that were possible. But more to the point—her cousin, Eliza! Would you believe that the man, who is indeed all affability wherever he goes, yet ever retains something of the sober scientist, a man who seems chronically to have a little aloofness mixed into his cordiality, that such a man, in short, is now shewing signs of being very likely to be soon very much in love?

Can it be possible? I am all astonishment. Oh, I know, I know, why should I be astonished? Only that if I had a cousin like his, sharing my house...

I blush to imagine such a scenario, even now; a warm languor grips my limbs. To not have the burden of being ever prevented to meet in private; to be able to finish our conversations without fear of being overheard, of being frowned upon for withdrawing too long from the rest of the company; to be like we were in October, when Mr Collins was off to Canterbury, those two otherworldly weeks that culminated in—Oh! Dear Tom, much as I love my sister, you are welcome to her; you could have a hundred Marias, if I could have but the one Ailsa Reid. Such a treasure within your reach, and you fall victim to a sweet, innocent, willy-nilly girl, infinitely her inferior in strength of mind and wisdom?

There is no reckoning with the sex. I should be relieved, naturally. He would be a fine match for my sister. But what would become of Ailsa?

*

Saturday morning. We have been invited to take tea at the doctor's, and William must needs accompany us. I could think of no reason to plant in his mind for not coming along. What a deceitful gardener am I. Indeed, I used to have no qualms of the sort before I was in fact guilty. Now, every little injustice I do him weighs on me, reminds me of how little I deserve the convenience of his protection. And so he must come, and I must be Mrs Collinsed for the day. At least Maria will call me Charlotte, or mortify me with her 'Lotty'.

*

Night. I doubt not that my pen is scribbling away tonight in unison with my sister's. She will be writing to Kitty, the flesh and blood version of Kitty, whereas I can write but to the idea of my Elizabeth. I do not begrudge her this freedom. Ever since I cleaved you thus in two, it has been unthinkable that I should pour out the entire contents of my heart to you. My reserve has not stemmed from either of our marriages, dear. It has a much deeper root than that.

But away with such thoughts! I have too much to tell to dwell on what is past and unchangeable. For there is something I must write of that has thrown me into a state of confusion. Perhaps that is why I am visited, more than common, by the ghosts of Decisions Past. A rift has been made in the fabric of my very existence, and I must, once more, decide whether I shall go through the hole or mend it, as I have had occasion to do before.

Ailsa and Dr Reid received us very amiably in the parlour, a room which neither Maria nor Mr Collins, it appeared, had ever set foot in before. Her I had called into my rooms in the morning to prepare for what was to come; for even if I suspected that Tom would be ready to forgive her any ladylike fainting fits as further proof of her niceness and 'charming qualities', I doubted whether Ailsa would be likewise impressed.

My sister carried herself off admirably, though mainly, I noted, through focusing narrowly on the tea set, which she praised—and won herself the good opinion of Lilly—and on the view onto the street, which seemed to gratify Dr Reid.

As for William, he was ill at ease among the morbid paraphernalia, and more than once I saw his gaze drawn to the box marked *tibiae*, as if he expected every moment the bones to burst out of their confinement and accost him.

He rallied himself to join in Maria's admiration for the tea set, adding that it reminded him of the beautiful collection Lady Catherine lets Mrs Jenkinson use as her own, in her snug apartment next to the servants' quarters; a comment that twisted Lilly's smile at Maria's compliment into a grimace, which, after a look from her mistress, she hid by simply leaving the room to fill up a tray of sweetmeats.

I dared not catch her eye and offer an apologetic smile, as would have been my inclination but two weeks ago. Despite Ailsa's assertion that Lilly's worries are solely founded upon concern about her mood swings, my heart shrinks at the dim look of distaste in her eyes. What does she know? What are the charges she lays against me? And could any of them really be more damning than the truth?

But—

As our visit wore on, Dr Reid invited us to peruse his modest library, small though it was, as he added bashfully. Maria was exceedingly pleased to find an old pianoforte in that room, and was soon prevailed upon to entertain us with her playing.

I sat in the window seat looking out onto 'Lilly's cherry tree', as we have called it ever since...and was soon joined, as I had both hoped and dreaded, by Ailsa.

"Musical too!" she said in a low voice, her proximity in this room filled with others, thrilling and provoking me unspeakably. "Tom shall have to take care, or he is in danger of being as infatuated with the one sister as I am with the other."

I felt my cheeks grow hot and turned my head to look out onto the dreary browns of the late autumn vegetation, hoping that neither William nor Dr Reid were observing us. The latter, I suspected, would be consummately employed in praising Maria's alacrity, and the former, I prayed, would be too wrapped up in acting the sparring partner to his host to pay any heed to what his wife might be doing.

Ailsa pressed her leg to mine, leaning closer on the pretence of sharing my interest in the uninspiring vista without. She smiled at my blushing confusion.

"I long for you," she whispered, and the tone of her voice left little room for me to doubt the meaning of her words. Not that I could—I felt the same, with every fibre of my being.

"I wish—" I said and broke off, for I did not rightly know what to wish for. That I had not married? What difference would it make if I were single? If I had been Miss Lucas, I would be at Meryton now, an old maid, pining away for... "I wish that we could be alone together." I finished my sentence inanely.

Ailsa placed a hand over mine, and I closed my eyes as a jolt of warmth shot through me. It was torture, torture for the both of us. I could not wish it to be otherwise.

"I have something I have been burning to tell you, and I must speak frankly. Our opportunities are too scarce for me to do otherwise. Do you remember that I had a letter last Tuesday? It was from my parents' solicitor at Edinburgh. My solicitor, I should say, for so he terms himself now."

I looked at her blankly.

"Surely you must remember, Charly?" she insisted, a teasing note to her voice, a gratified glint in her eyes. I racked my addled brain as she continued to caress my palm, sending small shoots of minute pleasure up my arm.

"Your inheritance!" I just managed to stop myself from exclaiming, as Maria, serendipitously, banged out the crescendo of 'Rondo à la Turque'.

Ailsa's smile widened, her gaze suddenly earnest, almost shy.

"I find myself recast overnight from the role of beggarly dependent to a woman of a not inconsiderable fortune."

"Oh! Ailsa, that's wonderful!"

She dipped her head.

"I am happy to be able to give Tom his bachelor freedom back, especially at a time when it seems he is ready to lay that freedom down as a sacrifice at such a worthy woman's feet. I will take up possession of my estate in Switzerland in a few months' time. My plan is to take up residence there, indefinitely."

"Switzerland?"

I felt as though a chasm had opened within me. Switzerland. Indefinitely. Perhaps to visit her cousin no more than once a year, at the most. To go into hiding from a world which had used her atrociously, yes; but also, to go away from me.

How could she look upon me so cheerfully? Did she not understand that she was tearing my very heart from my chest? How could I have allowed myself—once more—to be trifled with, to be cast aside as a used-up plaything, when Opportunity came knocking at the door?

My features, I knew, were arranging themselves into an impenetrable mask. I could not weep; I could not give vent to the misery which was building up in me every moment, in that room with my sister and her budding admirer, my husband, my...

"Lucas."

Childishly, I would not look at her; I feared that doing so would be tantamount to losing what little composure I could yet muster.

"Lucas, will you please look at me? I cannot propose to a woman who will not condescend to meet my gaze."

I stared at her then, my face, I cannot doubt, as silly as a goose's. Her cheeks bore the sweet pinkish tint of those rosebuds she had brought me; the wings of her nose fluttered as she drew breath. But her eyes, Eliza! Little did I think I would ever have the honour of being beheld in such a way, of being endearingly encompassed, inclosed—held and enspirited—of being shewn, without a shred of doubt, every recess of her soul. It was as if she had offered me the keys to a kingdom.

And then she did.

"Leave him," she breathed. "Leave him and come with me. Be mine."

Hunsford Parsonage
November, 1815

I broke off my narrative yesterday, which was very artful of me, you would say, Elizabeth—and you would be right. But such was the impact of her proposition upon me that all else seemed to have become as nothing around us. Would that it had been so.

For how can I accept of such a proposal, even if every selfish, throbbing part of me cries out an ecstatic 'Yes!'? If it were only Mr Collins to consider—but even him, my unfortunate, narrow-minded, self-important husband, I owe better than that. He has never behaved dishonourably by me. He does not love me—true, beyond a doubt; but he has ever valued me, after his fashion. I went into the marriage without any romantic pretensions or hopes, without any expectations—on that count, at any rate. But William is not my principal reason for rejecting an offer—such an offer! How much more convenient it would be if I had relatives like Ailsa's, a family who deserved nothing but scorn and desertion, who could make no claim to filial duty, who had forfeited even a common, disinterested fellow regard.

I cringe at my own ramblings. Has Ailsa lived through persecution, only to have it cast back in her face as something which facilitates her courage to go her own way? For shame, Charlotte Lucas! Mrs Collins. Oh!

My ink is mottled with tears—of frustration, anger, self-accusations. Perhaps, if Maria were to be really married... But how can I contemplate ruining everyone's reputation, everyone's hopes of future happiness, of comfort and security in life?

And yet, a small, nagging voice inside me insists, a voice that grows to a booming roar whenever *she* is near: How can I not?

How can I deny myself, deny *her*—this brave, completely captivating creature, this wonder of a person, whose mind and soul, whose very existence has brought me back to life from the limbo of mourning, whose presence I have come to depend upon for my spiritual sustenance, my soul's nourishment, my heart's delight?

Oh, what a wretch am I! What an unsolvable riddle is this life. To be beset from every quarter by duties and obligations, to the point of self-annihilation!

But then, when Ailsa touches her lips to mine, how sweet, how simple it all seems, how bearable the unbearable, if I could but have this.

Hunsford Parsonage
November, 1815

Dearest Lizzy,

I have just written a long epistle to you of Maria's stay here, and of the interest which she seems to have inspired in our man of medicine. Of this I can write to you, the real you, with comparable freedom. It will entertain you, I think, during the long hours you spend caring for your newly born baby girl; her brother, I doubt not, beset with jealousy—that first, all-encompassing pang. Being an oldest child myself, I feel for him, though I have no hesitation but that he will come to love her as ardently as ever your husband dotes upon his Georgiana.

As I dote upon my siblings.

You will wonder, my mind's Lizzy, whether I am keeping my heart's beloved in suspense?

I do not. Or rather, there was no possibility of further discussion, no opportunity for joint reflection, for which I could have wished; for who else in the world could I speak of it to but the lady herself? I pressed her hand. I could not, for the life of me, do anything else. Your sense of justice would find fault with me for this—as do mine, most heartily. But the way she shone, the way she radiated pleasure and happiness, after all her arduous afflictions! How cruel a fate that I cannot live up to that gesture of implicit promise. Do you remember how, when we were children, I used to preach: we create our own fate? What an insupportable little Know-All was I! That you could have put up with me, Eliza. I am forever indebted to you. Truly I am.

*

Tuesday night. We are just back from Rosings. Lady C. is set on her scheme for Bath, and Miss de Bourgh, in her vague way, seems rather to approve of it. We are destined now to spend Christmas in that town, which poses an obstacle for William, for he cannot very well entrust his chaplain with the whole responsibility for the Christmas and New Year's services on so short a notice.

Her ladyship's mind is made up, however, and we must all adjust our sails to allow for her course. I hear your laughter, Lizzy. Sparkling, vivacious, infectious—Oh! I do miss you most dreadfully when my spirits are low. Your sardonic smile, your 'philosophies', could ever take the brunt off sharp reality.

Hunsford Parsonage
November, 1815

Maria has come to confide in me. She was to pass a fortnight here this time, for our mother needs her back to prepare for the December festivities, and—more importantly—to keep the young ones in check. All aflutter, she wondered if it might be possible for me to prevail upon my husband to allow her back in January, or February, she added thoughtfully, if we should be in Bath until then.

I could not forego teasing her a little.

"You have taken a liking to Kent," I said, keeping my attention fixed on my needlework. I was mending one of the altar cloths, which has been attacked by heathen mice.

"Oh! Yes," she exclaimed and put her hands to her mouth. "That is to say…"

Her voice trailed off and she fretted at the hem of her gown. Reflexively, my eyebrows rose as she pulled a thread loose.

"I mend my own gowns nowadays, Lotty," she said, a touch of the five-year-old's truculence to her tone, and I laughed and loved her for it—for reading my mind, for her childish mien, her generous heart, even for that silly pet name she favours.

"So you do," I agreed and put my needlework aside, clasping her skittish hands in mine. "He's a fine man. I love him dearly. And I will but love him better the day you tell me he is to become my brother."

"Oh, Lotty! But on so short an acquaintance—" She flushed and could not finish her sentence.

I thought back, Lizzy, on all the ridiculous things I have uttered upon the subject of marriage, all the witticisms which you have tolerated, on your own behalf as well as upon Jane's, and then my own match of convenience—and I was silent.

"How odd that I should never have noticed him before," Maria reflected, for despite her maidenlike reluctance, she was by no means finished on the topic.

My heart went out to her. If I could have confided— but married women do not confide.

"We have not been much in company with him, my dear. Before the arrival of Miss Reid..."

"Oh, but she is a charming creature! Do you know she entertained me no end last night with the most singular stories of T—of Dr Reid as a boy? He looked gravely upon her, but it is evident how dear she is to him. I'm glad. I like her excessively."

Her countenance was all gleeful innocence, but she must have taken notice of the shadow that crossed over me, for she interrupted herself, her brow knitted.

"Do not you like her, Charlotte? Is there something..."

I smiled wanly, my heart too full for words. Distractedly, I went back to my needlework, if only for something to fix my eyes upon, to hide myself from my younger sister's suddenly penetrating gaze.

"I like her," said I, as I pushed the needle through the cloth, pricking my finger on the other side. I had forgotten my thimble.

I love her, echoed in my ears, ringing through me as if it would out, out at any cost.

I put my finger in my mouth, to stem the blood.

Volume Two

Bath
December, 1815

Dear Eliza,

We are arrived. I have written a hundred letters to you over the last week—during our preparations for the journey, on the road, as we were installed here—but none of them, as it were, preserved by paper and ink. This might be as well, for they have all been regurgitations on the same theme, and my escritoire is filling up with the unspoken. But here we are, at long last, and I am sitting locked in my closet, writing to you, before I join my husband in our bedchamber.

Yes, a joint bedchamber in Lady Catherine's rented townhouse, and I dread it more than if I had been asked to share my quarters with one of the servants.

I fret, worse than I did on the night I lost my maidenhead. My soul is at war, a strange struggle between the shame I ought to feel, and the wayward resistance I do feel.

Ailsa is asleep a few doors down the corridor, and Dr Reid has the room two doors from hers. It is a large, ostentatious house—ample enough room for everyone; yet her ladyship's annoyance at the cost of keeping such a numerous party in tolerable comfort is plainly noticeable. Soon however, William and Dr Reid will share a hackney coach back to Hunsford to practice their respective professions, and then we shall be a party of ladies, who should be able, I dare say, to adjust the expense of our living quarters accordingly.

William himself has pressed me to stay, as he is loath to leave the de Bourghs unattended by *any* Collinses. I made some feeble expostulations, asking whether he would be quite at ease at the rectory on his own, but my own hypocrisy stayed my tongue.

Oh, that he would be gone presently!

Tomorrow, we are to take the waters at—

Stay. There is a knock at the servant's entrance.

*

I have returned to my writing. My husband is fast asleep. Asleep while his wife, on the other side of the wall—

It was Ailsa at the door. Part apparition, part celestial harbinger in her night habiliment, a candle to light her way in her hand, her hair flowing down her back in shiny ringlets. There was something wild in her eyes, something awful, which might have frightened me in any other eyes but hers.

As soon I had let her in she pressed against me, pressed me up against the wall behind us, her lips on mine even before the door was firmly closed. My pulse boomed in my ears; my eager arms came about her. To hold her at last! How many weeks has it been? I shivered as I remembered that fateful day in the vestry, William's steps on the other side of the door coming closer, as I... I tore my lips away, reluctantly.

She shook her head, leading me over to the velvet and mahogany seat in the centre of the small room. As we sat, wrapped in a tight embrace, she whispered savagely:

"No, Charly, I will not allow it. You shall be mine in this house, even if I have to steal and lie and commit the blackest sins to make it so. Do not go to him. Do not go to him before you have been with me."

There was a heart-rending pain to her passion, and I felt myself go limp and weak and ready to yield to her every wish, gladly, without question. I could think of no words to still the fury of jealousy emanating from her; words would be futile, dishonest. I took her face between my hands and kissed her, kissed her with all my heart, with all the promises which my body alone could make, and drew her on top of me, luxuriating in the warm weight of her as I lay back against the arm of the seat.

She gasped and forced her leg between mine. I parted my thighs to make room for her. I doubt not but that she felt me through the thin fabric of my nightgown—felt my readiness, my acceptance which fairly equalled the violence of her need. Remorse welled up in her eyes, and she crumbled on top of me.

"Oh, Charly, what am I doing? I am no better than these accursed—"

"No, Ailsa. I implore you." I lifted myself to pull the frustrating layers of cloth out of the way, lifted her hand to my lips and kissed it tenderly. I caught her gaze and held it as I placed her fingers on me, and relished the rekindled fire that chased across her cheeks.

I nodded. I raised my hips. She pushed into me and I shook, and angled myself to take her more fully inside. I would not look away. A smile broke through her tears, and she groaned and quickly muffled her lips with mine, mine with hers, as she began working on me in earnest. Her palm slapped wetly against me, in a way that should have been shocking, but which lit a thousand fires in me. Awkwardly, my fingers sought her out and began to rub at her through her own nightdress. The fabric was soaking, all but transparent, and must have chafed, but she fervidly pressed against my fingers, inviting them to a daring dance.

I cannot say which of us first succumbed to that sweet abandon, that pivotal point from which there is no return. How can I put it into words? Do you remember that concert in town you took me to, with the great virtuoso who played the Presto from Vivaldi's 'L'estate', with such furore that there were more than one fainting fit in the audience? Do you remember how he kept us spellbound, anxious for each mighty dip and turn of his bow, the notes tangible, visceral, seeming to touch and ignite our very skin where they went? And how we ached and yearned for—something, some release from our earthly shackles, some spiritual immanence, some alternate eternity that the music seemed to offer, beyond sense, beyond sound, beyond all but this sublime now, soon (*presto, presto!*) and we were all uplifted into this ethereal frenzy, and as the final movement faded we all fell: like angels, like leaves, like—as I meant to say all along—lovers.

It is not for me to say whether Mrs Darcy has experienced the like in the arms of her husband. But I know, dearest, as we sat blushing and reluctant to meet one another's eye, you felt the phantom of it in that audience, at that concert; as did I.

When we had spent ourselves, I wrapped Ailsa in my weakened arms and kissed her. The door to my bedroom—Mr and Mrs Collins's bedroom—did not open, no steps were heard, nothing intruded upon our stolen moments of bliss.

But now she is gone, I dawdle at my writing desk, cataloguing my breaches of conduct, my paltry morality, in the hopes that it will make the traces of my transport fade.

Oh, would that I could but rise out of this chair, put my pen away for the night, and go to share my true love's bed. Yes, I hear the cloying romanticism of that statement, Lizzy, and I know full well that, at least in part, I have only myself to blame for the leghold trap I find myself in. Did I not myself build the foundations on which it was laid out?

I ask only a comfortable home. No, I have not forgotten; my former words, thoughts and actions haunt me. They plague me to distraction.

And yet, if but for a few moments, I am content simply to sit here, as after the performance by the Vivaldi virtuoso, giving way to a quiet ecstasy, a listing, sensuous lassitude.

You see how I falter, Eliza. How I cannot even be adequately ashamed of myself. I must to bed, in the hope that my cuckolded husband will not be woken by the wanton pounding of my heart.

Bath
December, 1815

I am back at my pen, after a few days' interlude of exemplary behaviour to my husband and hostesses, to Dr Reid, to Lord This and Lady That about town—to everyone, in short, but to her whom it would delight me most to please.

The morning after that tumultuous (wonderful) first night, Mr Collins inquired after my whereabouts during those hours conventionally dedicated to repose, a queer look in his eye which I have not heretofore encountered. I dissembled as best I could, telling him I had fallen asleep on the seat in my closet, overcome with fatigue after the journey, which was, by halves, a species of truth.

I did fall asleep on the seat. I could not countenance going through to him after all, my whole being still aglow with her caresses. He is a short-sighted, buffoon-like man, Eliza, I grant you—but even he could not have failed to detect what was the matter with me.

I averted my gaze, squirming at his tone of displeasure. After we had joined the rest of our party, I contrived to pass Ailsa a billet telling her we must not meet in private while my husband remained under this roof.

I know the precise moment she read it, unfolding it in her napkin where she sat over by Mrs Jenkinson, for her brow darkened, and she excused herself shortly afterwards, much to Lady Catherine's dissatisfaction.

She has not spoken to me since. Oh, Lizzy, it makes me feel dead inside! Here we are, in such close quarters, and yet further apart even than when we were relative strangers to each other, that first, fateful night at Rosings Park. She should know—she must know how I despise him! How my skin crawls at the very thought of upholding my solemn vows. Why, then, will she torment me? Why will she make the difficult impossible?

I fear desperation shall make me imprudent. I cannot help thinking, if she should chuse to leave with Dr Reid and my husband for Hunsford tomorrow...

It is time to go and take the waters. I will return to this doleful scrawling anon.

*

Night. We have been to take the waters for the fourth time in as many days since our arrival, and much to my surprise, Miss de Bourgh is looking the better for it. Perhaps there is, as the popular opinion goes, something fulsome, at least, about the air here; even though it appears smoky and disagreeable to a country madam like myself. I cannot otherwise account for it, as the water itself is rank and turgid. It leaves a coat around the tongue and the inside of one's cheeks, which lingers well into evening. I have taken to sipping at it daintily as I receive it under the watchful eye of Lady C.; as soon as she is looking elsewhere, I hastily empty my cup back into the well. William has caught me at it, once or twice, his mouth and forehead creasing in disapprobation.

Well, if he will make himself sick in order to please his patroness, that must stand for him. Besides, he will be going back to prepare for the Christmas and New Year's service on the morrow, while I have to remain where I am: the sacrificial lamb to her ladyship's whims.

You hear that I am not as distraught as I previously gave myself reason to be. I have spoken to Ailsa. After our evening meal, she withdrew, as she announced, in order to pack her things, and this induced me to break my own prohibition against our meeting tête-à-tête. As soon as I could, without arousing suspicion, I retired and went, brashly, desperately, directly to her door. I believe I must have been white as a sheet, my limbs stiff with vexation, for when she opened the door, her countenance fell, and she ushered me inside, looking hastily about her.

She sat me on the seat in front of the vanity, and her dear hands stroked my face and hair.

"Lucas, you do not look well! Pray tell me what is the matter? Do you need my cousin's attention? Oh, truly, my love, you look—is it your hemicrania? Shall I call for hot water? I should have some herbs with me; I brought them especially..."

I made an abortive gesture, but she turned to rummage through her trunks, which, I observed in horror, she had already prepared for departure. A noise rose in my throat. I could not prevent it.

"Please, Ailsa! Oh, please, do not leave me!"

She peered at me in surprise, a parcel of mending lace in her hand dropping back into the trunk.

"Leave you?" She let the lid slip back into place and came up to me, her expression worried as she began to turn my head this way and that, her eyes carefully examining mine. "Charly, are you hallucinating? I am right here; I was just a few feet away. Is your vision blurred? Do you have spots before your eyes?"

"I am... I meant tomorrow. Is there nothing I can do to convince you to stay? I entreat you, command me to do what you will!"

I was pulling at her gown, rumpling her skirt as if I had been a child wildly protesting to regain her mother's favour. Ailsa peered down on me in confusion.

"Why, I had no notion that you felt so strongly about my staying in these rooms. I did not think it was worth the quarrel with her ladyship to refuse quitting them. Tom's quarters are a bit further down the hall, 'tis true, but... Really, my dear, why do you upset yourself so? What does it matter which rooms I reside in nominally, when you must know I plan to be in yours as much as I can without causing any too well-founded gossip among the servants?"

My head reeled. I had to put my face in her skirts to stop a maniacal laughter from bursting forth with the abrupt release of tension. All in vain. I laughed. I cried. Ailsa dropped to her knees, embracing me.

"I thought you were going back." I hiccoughed into her neck, the patch of exposed skin so infinitely comforting, infinitely precious to me. "I thought you were going back with Tom and my—Mr Collins. I thought you were leaving."

She looked at me incredulously, the tips of her fingers wiping tears off my cheeks, her mouth a questioning circle. Her forehead creased.

"Why on earth...?" she demanded at length.

"You've been so cold and perturbed ever since... You have barely uttered a syllable to me."

I blushed at the pettishness in my voice and touched her hand imploringly. Her visage had darkened the way it had upon reading my note, and my chest constricted.

"Pray do not be angry with me. I have longed for you more than I thought humanly possible—these last few days—"

My voice would not hold. She made a guttural sound and clasped me to her, as if she would fain have attached me to her in a way that admitted of no separation.

"You are a fool, a damned fool, as less well-bred gentlemen would say, Lucas. Did it never occur to you that I might be avoiding you from a surfeit of love, rather than from a lack thereof? Have I not been acting according to *your* instructions, rather than after the bidding of my own heart? I cannot do things by halves. These last days, knowing that you lay down by him each night, while during the day you have been the life and soul of the party—my dearest, loveliest—Oh! It has been intolerable. I could not... I cannot abide it! If I have been out of sorts, have I not had reason to be? To give way to a nincompoop, to a prating knave, who has been given, by no virtue of his own, the greatest honour a fellow could wish to have bestowed upon him: the title of your husband, with all the sweet obligations and duties, the lawful rights that this title entails? What is a duke, an earl, the prince regent himself to Mr Collins?"

She broke off, her eyes moist with inflamed frenzy, her breast heaving with her impassioned speech. Oh,

Lizzy—if ever there was such a thing as a noble jealousy, Miss Ailsa Reid is surely the most shining example thereof! My bosom ached to think that I had inadvertently caused her this pain. I parted my lips to speak, but she put her fingers to them to stem the flow.

"Stay," she whispered, her eyes glazed yet warm with affection, humbled, as it were, by her own fierceness. "Oh, stay, my love. I am guilty of the basest emotions when I should, and rightly so, be the most forbearing. To know that I have secured your affections, even if only a sliver of space in your heart, should make me glory in my good fortune, not rail against those who have but a theoretical claim to them. Can you forgive my possessive spirit? And yet forgiveness won't do, for it implies that I should seek to be otherwise, and it is impossible; I cannot be the virtuous, saintly heroine of one of your popular novels; I cannot give you up for the sake of prudence, of convention, of pre-existing claims, either in the eyes of the world or God! I may be a sinner doomed to the Eternal Fires, but I am an honest one, if so. I won't be a scheming adulteress. I won't call my love by any other name, while you remain the legal wife and property of a man. I must have you or lose you completely. If these last days of torment have taught me anything, it is the indivisibleness of my rakish heart. Tell me you will come with me to Switzerland, Lucas. Tell me anew. For if you will not, I must needs go. You do see that, do you not? You see that it is impossible for me to stay and watch this travesty of a husband of yours trespass daily on those territories of intimacy where I would fain stake my irrevocable claim? Call me a usurper, if you will. Rue the day you met with such an implacable spirit. But be mine. Be mine fully, in every sense, or send me on my way."

She fell back, exhausted by her own outpouring, but still her eyes gleamed and smouldered as she regarded me, as if she would have liked to throw caution to the wind and ravish me then and there. This way she has of looking at me—it charms and disarms me, until I would consent to anything simply to stay wrapped up in her adoring gaze.

I tried to steel myself, to think soberly upon the topic at hand. And yet sense, sobriety, sacrifices, making-do—for what, Lizzy? For the sake of my dead child? For a husband who has all but purchased me, more than partly, as a toy for his insipid tyrant of a patron? For my gossiping mother, my braggart of a father, my giddy, beloved siblings?

"My family—"

I could not continue. I needed not. I saw that she understood me. The light went out of her eyes.

There was no other way I could more effectually have become acquainted with my heart's overarching concern. I offered her my hand. I fell to my knee.

"Ailsa Reid, I am yours, if you will have me. I am but yours. Only, let me... Would you help me think of some way to extricate myself from the situation I have landed myself in, while causing the least possible pain to those whose interests are necessarily intertwined with mine? This is my only qualm, Ailsa. My one, inviolable obligation. You would not wish to ruin Tom's chances of happiness, his standing in polite society, for the sake of your own, however dear, designs. I know you would not. Your loyalty is part of what I love about you. Of what you are. Would you have me with this caveat, my darling? I ask too much, I know. I care not for my own reputation. I would throw it away this instant, if no one but myself were concerned therein. But think of Maria. Think of Tom. Think of my filial duties; you would not have me err in these as glaringly as ever your devilish uncle, if for a better cause? I do not know how we shall go about it. I know it is impossible for me to come to you with a perfectly clear conscience. But when I do, I intend to come to you for life. For the sake of our future life together, dearest, let us find a way to spare our relations as much as possible. And pray, do not leave me to be Mrs Collins to the end of my days without you!"

She gripped my hands, pulling me from my knees and up into her arms. We were a tangled mess of straining lips, petticoats and tears. As our embrace deepened into ardour, a bottle fell off her vanity and rolled across the carpet towards the door, spreading a cloud of a powderish substance about it.

My lips stopped on their trail, at the sound of...something. Ailsa stilled in my arms. Again the sound came, and now there was no denying it: sneezing, loud but growing fainter, as if the person from whence it came were moving hastily away. I stared at the door. In our distraction, we had not closed it completely.

I hung back, my complexion, I doubt not, returned to that horrid pallor which had startled my beloved thus upon my first entering her chambers. Her expression mirrored my own dreadful consternation. Then, out of the blue, her brow cleared, her eyes softened, a peculiar little smile chased across her rosy, kiss-stung lips.

"I think," said she, slowly, thoughtfully, "I think this may not be cause for such great an alarm as one would at first assume."

"Why, Ailsa—"

She shook her head and lifted my hand to her lips.

"You must return to your rooms, in case I am mistaken, love. But I dare say I am not. Even so, I would not let anything imperil our happiness in days to come, as you say, when happiness is just within our reach."

I must have looked as though I thought she had lost her senses, for she laughed (as sweet and pearly a laughter as you ever heard, Elizabeth—Oh! that you could meet this charming girl, this part angel, part emboldened adventuress; she would have your affection within the hour, your unswerving regard in the space of a day or two) and rose to accompany me to the door.

Leaning in to take leave for the night, her lips were pressed to the shell of my ear as she spoke, *sotto voce*:

"I believe it was Mrs Jenkinson. No, do not be alarmed. She will not give us away, Charly; she is of our party, you must know. She is one of us."

She is one of us. The words rang through me as I made my way back to my closet, to pour out my heart and find solace in these pages. There can be no two interpretations of this. But to think—part of me balks at the idea—to think that Mrs Jenkinson, Mrs Jenkinson whom I have lived in such close proximity to for these past years—seen every week—taken every conceivable repast with! And that Ailsa, in the space of a few months... What does Mrs Jenkinson know? And if she but suspected before, surely now—that telltale sneeze! Have I been intentionally blind? But nothing, nothing at all, has led me to believe... All these years, for Lady Catherine de Bourgh to have put the charge of her daughter into the hands of... I know not what to think. My thoughts, as you see, are all in disarray, filled with stops and starts, sputtering with incredulity. My wits are scattered. Mrs Jenkinson! And what will she do?

Yet, I confess, my dear, long-lost Eliza (for so you are to me), I go to bed tonight a happy, reckless creature. My darling loves me. She will not desert me, despite my silly apprehensions, my frail heart. And is it possible that we might find a way to be together? Dare I hope? We are chasing a dream, you would say, ever-sensible Lizzy, but yet, in my heart of hearts, give me leave to imagine that you would wish me well. Let me rest a while. Let me sleep. Let me not wake up from this gold-spun fiction to harsh, intractable reality.

> *And this weak and idle theme,*
> *No more yielding but a dream,*
> *Gentles do not reprehend.*
> *If you pardon, we will mend.*

I lowered my head.

"None, madam," I returned, not trusting my voice to give a finer speech on the occasion.

"Miss Reid?"

"I am as obliged to you as to Mrs Collins's kind condescension, your ladyship. Very much so."

I dared not look at her, Elizabeth. Even the warmth of promise in her tone sent delicious thrills down my spine.

"It is settled then," her ladyship proclaimed, and the whole party, it seemed to me, fell back in a joint exhalation of bated breaths.

It was decided that we should go and take the waters in an hour from thence; just enough time for the servants and Ailsa to move her ready-made trunks and bundles into my rooms—*our* rooms. I was sitting as if upon needles the whole time, barely able to look up from the book I was pretending to read, for fear that I should expose myself in front of the footmen. My heart palpitated. The blood rang in my ears, bloomed across my cheeks; in short, my infamous composure hung on a threadbare string, to which I dared not introduce any additional pressure. I trained my eyes on the text in front of me as though my life depended upon committing the verse to memory. I could make no sense of it. A maid asked where ma'am would like her toilette laid out, and Ailsa replied that she should leave everything on the vanity and withdraw, she would lay it out herself, thank you, Hannah.

Of course Ailsa knew the maid's name. She knows everyone's name in this house, I dare say; it is just her way. Whereas, I could not even preserve equanimity enough to read a book, let alone engage in idle banter with the people around us. I sighed and took to mouthing the words on the page to myself, in an effort to seem— preoccupied, at least.

"Are you reading Donne?"

She was at my side, the heat emanating from her making my head spin. I dared not look up. I nodded, blushing as I stumbled over an intricate rhyme.

Ailsa bent down and brushed her lips across my cheek. I all but jumped out of my skin.

"There's no one here, Lucas," she murmured, amused. Her eyes glittered.

"Oh, you devil!" I exhaled, pulling her to me for a proper kiss.

She laughed, her mouth warm and half open, her hands pressed to my chest, part entreating, part holding me back.

"Hannah has promised to return presently to help us prepare for her ladyship's excursion. We must be ready in a quarter of an hour, if you can tear yourself away from your reading."

I could have pinched her for her teasing—pinched her or kissed her, I knew not which—but we both heard Hannah's quick steps through Elna corridor, and stood, abruptly, as one, my book falling to the floor. Ailsa stooped to pick it up, handing it back to me with a flourish, her finger pointing conspicuously to the line

breast to breast, thigh to thigh

I scowled disapprovingly; it was all I could do to keep from swooning in front of the maid. Ailsa laughed again, innocently, heartily, as if I had just shared the most diverting pleasantry with her. She turned to Hannah waiting uncertainly at the door and exclaimed:

"Right on time! What a treasure you are, Hannah."

The maid coloured and curtseyed, her embarrassment, I realise in retrospect, successfully masking my own.

*

If you would believe it, Eliza, the evening's entertainment was provided by Mrs Jenkinson; the lady in question proves not unskilled at the pianoforte, her fingers—I noted with a slight flush which could be explained away, I hope, by the warm blackberry wine we were imbibing—are uncommonly nimble for a woman of her age. We withdrew at an earlier hour than we have been used to while the gentlemen resided with us, claiming a need to adjust to the change in our living arrangements.

Lady Catherine did not seem displeased. I fear she had been drowning her sorrow at the loss of her most attentive beau (if, indeed, such a term could ever be applied to that gentleman) in a touch too many glasses of wine than even her sturdier frame could carry. In truth, she is surprisingly healthy for an old crone—there, I said it, Lizzy; you would be shocked and entertained by my plumpness.

No sooner had we left the parlour than Ailsa linked her arm through mine, conjuring up in my mind that stormy night at the doctor's—a lifetime ago, it seems, though it has been but a few months!—when first she made me hers.

I put my hand over hers, my insides aflame with anticipation, and led her up the stairs. She had no occasion to signal me which way to turn at the top of them; this time, I knew precisely where I was going.

"Hannah?" I murmured, as I quietly slipped open the door and admitted my love inside.

"I told her we would not require her services for the rest of the night. I hope I was not too forward, Charly, I—"

I turned the key in the lock and backed her up against the door, ravenous as a starving man in the desert, confronted with a sumptuous feast.

"Miss Reid," I remonstrated in a low, raspy voice that seemed at once foreign and truer to my heart's yearning than my more sedate, ordinary timbre, "all day you have stoked the fires in me, adding wood after tantalising wood whenever I have painstakingly regained my wherewithal. And now you play the blushing maiden? Fie on you, madam. I crave. I hunger. I am run mad!"

All affectation fell from her then, and she placed her hand on my glowing cheek, coming closer; the creped satin of her gown rustled where it touched and rubbed against my muslin.

"Run mad as often as you chuse, Lucas," she quipped. "But do not faint!"

I laughed—a giddy, delirious laugh—and pulled her to me, all but carrying her over to my bed. Our bed. The bed we are to share, from here on, with the full approbation of Lady Catherine de Bourgh.

Come, you would have laughed, too, all things considered, Eliza. I know you would.

Slowly, as if in silent agreement that we would savour each moment of this first night together, we began to undress, helping each other unbutton, unlace, unbind. With every article of clothing that fell to reveal more of her perfectly smooth, milky-white skin, so pale it seemed almost iridescent by the light of our single candle, I felt a sparkling excitement billow through me, as were I growing intoxicated on a golden French wine. Every part of her seemed dear to me. Every dip and curve exquisitely formed, but more so, in truth, because they were hers, and she, by her own free will—through a consent that appeared more sacred to me than any sham marriage vows drawn up between parties who have neither mind nor inclination to be committedly devoted to one another—mine. I stood before my true bridal bed, Lizzy, and I trembled. Up until I met Miss Ailsa Reid, my soul and body have never been joined in such perfect harmony to the respect of and doting upon one fellow creature. I would die for her, as the poets say, though their meaning has always been lost on us; for would I not, in death, cause pain of the most atrocious kind where I would the least wish to harm? No, I cannot wish for the vainglory of dying *for* her, though were she but more of the angel, which her grace leads me to compare her to, I could say that I would die—gladly, sweetly—to be *with* her. But she is flesh, glorious though mortal as mine, and so we must find a way—if there were but a way—

"You look grave, Lucas."

I smiled, though my affliction must have shone through my expression, for she shook her head, making her free-flowing tresses of hair dance about her naked shoulders and sweep across her bared chest.

"Less thinking, more doing. Come to bed."

My heart leapt as she lifted the counterpane to slip underneath.

"No!" I burst out, and she stopped, surprised, halfway into bed. My face warmed at my lascivity, but I carried on—I had to—with my request: "I would prefer... That is to say, unless you are very cold..."

Ailsa looked at me, confounded. Then her face relaxed into understanding, a slow smile creeping across her lips.

"I am not so very cold." She smoothed the counterpane back and lay on top of it, on her side, facing me. "And I trust you to keep me warm enough, for all that."

I lay beside her. She folded me in her arms and came close, as in that piece of verse: *breast to breast, thigh to thigh*, and I felt the ferocious longing which had beset me all day once more overtake me. I welcomed it.

"I want to kiss you," I breathed nonsensically between kisses, as her deft hands lit an all but agonising yearning wherever they went.

"You are kissing me." Her eyes sparkled with mirth, but also a reflection of my own growing need.

"No, I mean, yes, but—I want to kiss you everywhere."

"Everywhere?" Her eyebrows lifted.

"Yes, everywhere, everywhere. May I?"

Gorgeous pink flowered down her neck and shoulders as she sucked in her breath and pulled my face to hers. She nodded into her kiss. I would not—I could not—settle for such a mute concession, such a *yielding* to my passion. I would not have her yield to me. She has yielded enough in her tenderer years.

"Would you like that, Ailsa? Tell me truly, for indeed—"

"Do." Her face was a dark tint of scarlet, her eyes wide and bottomless. "I want you everywhere. I want you to consume me; isn't that what they call it? To consummate a marriage? I want you to consummate the bond between us, Charly. I want every part of me to be made anew—by you."

I let out a sound in the region between a moan and a cry: an animal noise, which I would not have pronounced myself capable of. And then I was upon her—starving, craving, once again. My lips paid homage to her goddess face, her neck and shoulders; even behind her darling ears I touched my lips to her skin, every vein of mine a pulse as she shivered and sighed beneath me. Such sighs! I was drunk on those audible manifestations of her pleasure, spurring me on to ever bolder attempts.

Even now, on recollection, the blood pounds in my ears, I am almost faint to think—but I <u>will</u> write.

As I continued down her magnificently swelling bosom, her sighs intensified; her limbs were writhing, hands gripping the blanket beneath her and gathering it into her fists. I paused.

She lifted her head, her eyes hazy, her lips red and puffy as if she had been biting them.

"You are the loveliest thing I ever beheld," I pronounced solemnly.

"Please," she wheezed, and with that singular urgency in her voice she could have commanded an army to march gleefully, even into a doomed battle, merely for the pleasure of knowing that they had, each one of them, her full approval.

She needed not prevail on me twice. I put my lips back to their charming travail, mapping the impossibly silky expanse of her stomach. As I reached her navel, I flicked my tongue into its shallow depth, playfully, to tickle her, and she gasped and clutched my head.

She tasted sweet and salty in equal measure, and— Bless me! I wanted more.

I kissed a line down from her navel to that breathtaking cloud of auburn fuzz that stood watch over her most private region, and in that instant, addled by the powerful, rousing scent of her, I knew what I must do: what my hunger, my desire to fully experience every part of her bid me do.

I put my palms to her thighs and parted them. I let my eyes fall upon her and it was so unlike—

You know I have only ever seen—

Oh, but it was beautiful. A swollen bud of a sweet briar, glistening with dew, slowly undulating as my breath touched its delicate petals.

My mouth watered, and I had to swallow, twice.

"Ailsa—" I could not take my eyes from her; I could not even begin to put my request into comprehensible words. What words are there? Our language is sorely devoid of polite expressions for such peculiar instances as these.

"Yes." Her voice was tight as if a wire had been strung through her and wound until it was ready to burst. She cleared her throat. "Yes, Charly. Please do."

I put my lips to her, and the bloom unfurled.

*

The bloom unfurled. How vainly I struggle to portray the strange rapture that took hold of me, as I tumbled headfirst into this valley of wonders. How? What? The nib of my pen stumbles, leaks excesses of ink onto the page.

I kissed her. I kissed her there, and I could not stop kissing her, as the molten taste of her teased my lips, as she shifted and arched up to me. A gluttonous need made me deepen and extend my kisses; my tongue darted out, and I—

She convulsed, crumbled, her head turning frantically to sob into her pillow, and I knew that the wire had finally sprung loose. A gush of liquid oozed between her folds, and I lapped at it, humming into her flesh, as if it were the nectar of Heaven, issuing from the most hallowed of springs.

At last, I put my cheek to her and held her to me. She encircled me weakly, still crooning, sobbing, babbling softly. Madness! If this be madness, I want no part of sense. If this be sin, I profess myself a sinner, unrepentant, a heathen to the very quick.

If this be not who I was, then I cannot, I will not go back. For I am, quite simply, now and forever: Lucas, crowned and baptised by my beloved's balm.

Bath
December, 1815

Sweet Lizzy,

—For sweet is everything to me in these gilded days. I am afraid I had to put my pen down after my last effusions; Ailsa awoke, and I— Well.

Her curiosity, though, would not be abated until I had shewed her some of what I had written. She read, biting her finger and blushing handsomely as she came to my effort at depicting what passed between us during our first night in these rooms. I held out my hand to snatch the sheet of paper back from her, but she batted me away; for she would not be interrupted before reaching a resolution, she said. I was mortified. I fiddled with my pen, ruffling the vane with anxious fingers as she read on. At last, she put the sheet down with a sigh and closed her eyes briefly, a small shudder running through her. I folded up the paper and put it back in my escritoire, fishing up the key from within my stays to lock it away.

"You write well, Charly. You could have us hanged."

I sunk my head. "I am... I am heartily sorry, Ailsa; it is a habit, I—"

I knew she was right; it is not merely nonsensical to keep up this habit of mine. There is a real element of danger, which I have not let myself consider for fear of losing my only, albeit imaginary confidante.

Ailsa brushed her fingers over my stained knuckles. "Why, Lucas, I would not have you stop writing for the world! You have a real talent with your busy fingers, your quick ink. Perhaps when we are in Switzerland you could turn your hand to penning—Oh! I don't know, a Gothic romance?"

I laughed, yet my insides quaked.

"When we are in Switzerland..."

"Hush," she admonished, stealing into my ready embrace. "We shall find a way. We must. Let us be optimistic, my love. Just this once."

She kissed me fondly. I crushed her to me. She sighed against my lips.

"How would you like to be crowned again, my Queen of the Voluptuous Metaphors?"

*

Do you never complain to me about Bath again, Eliza! If you could but see it through a lover's eyes, you would admit that it is a seat worthy of Kings. What delightful aspects greet you, wherever you turn to take a stroll, the arm of your sweetheart wound through yours, her hip swinging against you, heating you, even through the abundant layers of your winter attire. The river Avon is prettily glazed and swirling underneath its thin sheet of ice. The handsome Pulteney Bridge shimmers with hoarfrost and is a sight to behold as you lean out across the embankment, dizzy with besotted joy.

Ailsa teases me relentlessly, but I maintain: there can be no place as gratifying to the discerning eye as Bath in

December. Mark my word! I shall copy this sentiment—with certain alterations and omissions—into my real letter to you.

We find ourselves to be a convenient contrivance for Mrs J. and Miss de Bourgh to leave the house unattended by either her ladyship or a host of footmen. We have fallen into a routine of going off with Lady Catherine to take the waters in the morning, after which the four of us leave her ladyship to be escorted back by her manservant while we linger in town on various pretexts, all of which we must remember to give some feigned evidence on our return. As soon as ever Lady C.'s equipage has rounded some obliging corner and we are safely out of sight, Mrs Jenkinson and her protégée wave to us, merrily, as they slip off to some unknown location or other, doing God knows what. I blush to think. Ailsa's eyes sparkle wickedly at supper as she observes how the waters, each and every day, seem to offer some new improvement to Miss de Bourgh's looks and health. Anne smiles back—yes, positively, Lizzy! The little waxen doll can smile!—remarking, in veiled tones, how this elixir is the only thing that can sustain her through the insupportable dullness of the winter months. On cue, her mother raises her glass to Bath. To Bath! We all join heartily in the toast.

I almost feel sorry for her ladyship in her blustering ignorance. If she only knew— But then, what is there to know? What can it be that they are doing here, which they might not do in the comfort of their own apartments at Rosings Park?

I put the question to Ailsa as we walked into our favourite tea room, not far from the Roman Baths.

"Oh, Charly, you are such an ingénue at times, despite your wiser years!"

I frowned. She leaned in close, on pretence of adjusting the frill cap under my bonnet, and whispered: "I do love that quality about you. I would not spoil it for the world!"

I sat down in the chair pulled out for me by an obsequious waiter and ordered our usual pot of Pekoe and plate of biscuits, impatiently waving him off. Ailsa smiled and thanked him.

"I do not know how you reconcile your newfound project of turning me into an authoress with your wishfulness to keep me in a state of ignorance as to the ways of the world."

I was close to sulking, shamefully enough. But you know it has always peeved me to be found wanting in knowledge—though I would certainly forbear experience—on any topic under discussion. Why would Mrs Jenkinson, whom I have lived so close to for nigh on three years, have taken Ailsa into this unprecedented confidence, and not me?

I am loath to admit that the question is easily answered. I am the rector's wife. And Ailsa—you would think me blinded by infatuation, I doubt not, but there is something about her open countenance, her earnest wit, her thoughtful acknowledgement of even the slightest, least consequential creature in her environs, which inspires an unheard-of confidence in her from the unlikeliest of quarters. If you will remember, she even had the dubious honour of procuring Lady Catherine de Bourgh's condescension (I will not call it approbation, for to have that would be to be reduced to the fawning insincerity of one I claim but too close a relation to) on but a short acquaintance. No, on proper introspection, I cannot blame Mrs J. for placing confidence where it ought to be placed. Still, I must have looked displeased enough, for Ailsa grasped my hand across the table, her eyes filled with concern.

"Do not be angry with me, Lucas. I assure you, this insight into matters has been foisted upon me most unwillingly. I—it took me a not inconsiderable amount of politics to be granted the knowledge of these two ladies' private affairs, while procuring myself the leave to abstain from joining in their activities, on the most solemn oath that I would not betray their trust."

I looked at her. I stirred my tea. I was silent.

"They—" Her voice faltered. She looked about her. "Really, my dear, this is not the place!"

"Oh, come, Ailsa," I tried to smile; truly my spirits were raised merely by this half admission. "Not a soul could hear us over this din. But you need not tell me. It is selfish of me to insist. And for what? Mere curiosity. I assure you, I am sincerely ashamed of myself. I just—well, I confess I was childishly affronted that you would not trust me as you do your own heart."

"Oh, Charly!"

I held up my hand.

"Pray do excuse me. My lips will be sealed on the subject from here on."

Ailsa pursed her own charming lips. I could see the internal debate playing out in her eyes before she leaned in anew and breathed in my ear:

"Miss Anne de Bourgh likes to have her bottom paddled by strange women every now and then. There's a sort of—a society—a sisterhood—I know not what. You may depend upon it, I have not inquired further into this matter. There. Now you know. All I require of you, my sweet, innocent parson's wife, is that you do not let your confusion shine too visibly in those great, big eyes of yours on our next encounter with these sprightly dames. If they suspected—"

You can imagine how I looked, Eliza. Look you yourself in the pier glass upon reading this (although you never, ever shall!), and you will have a fair emulation of my features on this occasion, I warrant.

"Oh, for Heaven's sake, Lucas!"

Ailsa's tone of voice was exasperated, though she could barely conceal her mirth. Our eyes met. We burst into girlish giggles, the tension of the revelation giving way to the release of a near-hysterical fit, and of this, in truth, more than one person in the tea room took notice, though the reason for it—upon my word!—shall be forever unknown to them.

Miss Anne de Bourgh likes—

That slap in the plum orchard—

Nay, but truly! Had I been writing a piece of fiction, I could not have invented anything—

I must lay down my pen.

Bath
December, 1815

Now that you have composed yourself, Elizabeth (the pot calling the kettle, and so forth), once more I dip my nib in ink to continue my narrative. Is that not a pretty name for my senseless outpourings? Calling it thus seems to lend an air of structure to my errant roamings, a sense—a hope—of a conclusion to come. Switzerland, Switzerland—we talk between us now of that distant, mountainous realm as the virtuous speak of that other kingdom, where they shall reap the rewards of their present toil. I think not that I may count myself among the virtuous anymore, in the strict doctrinal sense of the term. Yet I am wearied with contrition, wearied with guilt. I cannot wish for a Heaven where I would be forever parted from my soul's desire. I cannot love a God—

But enough, and too much, on this strain. My love bids me repose, for the present, in the assurance that we will find a solution. And so I will. If but for the sweetness of the present moment, I will.

You may well guess, Lizzy, that despite my good intentions, my best endeavours, I could not help but turn as rufous as the rose of Lancaster on our meeting Mrs Jenkinson and Miss de Bourgh that evening. That is to say, though I could not observe my own mien, the warmth on my skin and Ailsa's head shaking from right to left assured me I did not pass the test.

Mrs Jenkinson merely smiled thinly, as is her wont, and for an instant that strange—that outrageous—tableau flashed before me, of this pale, grey mouse of a woman, this governess turned lady-in-waiting, wielding an implement—I know not what: a flogger? A baker's peel? Before her prim and wan little Miss Anne, on her hands and knees, leaning upon cushions perhaps, her skirts hoisted up, a glint in her eye—that glint which, as I cast my mind back, I have observed before, but never, ever could I have...

"How do you do, Mrs Collins? Allow me to say, madam, you look unwell. Will you take some cordial? Perhaps a glass of mulled wine?"

"Allow me, Mrs Jenkinson."

Ailsa put the glass in my hand, her eyes shooting daggers, yet, at the same time, a smile played on her lips. Mrs Jenkinson curtseyed—a wry take on the servant's curtsey—and went to ladle up some wine for Anne.

"You are letting your imagination run away with you, Charlotte. This charming transparency of yours! But pray, do try to remember Lady Cat—"

"What are you two whispering about?" came her ladyship's interposition, uncannily on cue, and Ailsa, as ever, saved the day. She introduced the topic of silks, on which Lady Catherine, as on most subjects, holds strong opinions.

Gratefully, I drank my wine, trying to wash away the new and unbidden image of silks falling from my love's alabaster limbs, as I felt the burning sensation of Mrs Jenkinson's and Miss de Bourgh's eyes upon me from across the room.

*

Christmas morning. I have received an account from my husband of the pies which Travis has provided for the parish poor on my instructions. I could have done without this reminder of my neglected duties. He has taken pains with his handwriting, I see—no doubt expecting that his letter will be shewn to the person for whom it is primarily intended, his most-condescending (I quote) patroness. With all my heart, I shall gift her this piece of nonsense. Oh, but he puts me out of humour with myself!

A dusting of snow sits upon the window panes. We are readying ourselves to attend church, after which we are obliged to go to a dinner party, and probably we won't be allowed to come back until well past midnight, dead on our feet and ready to fall into bed to sleep the innocent sleep of worn-out saints, when I had much rather...

But here's Hannah to attend us. I doubt not that Christmas at Pemberley is a much more pleasant affair. And the boys will be back from school at Lucas Lodge. Would I rather be anywhere but here? Why no. One look at my bedfellow, my days' and nights' companion, is enough to strengthen me in my resolve to brave all irksome society that may be thrust upon us with equanimity. But Hannah—

*

A full three days have passed since last I held my pen in hand and yet I have very little of note to relate. I remember now but too well, Lizzy, your objections to Bath. These prattling curs! These gossiping dowagers! These silly maidens who deck themselves with silk flowers and outlandish laces, scuttling for prime position on the marriage market, content to be weighed up as so many pounds of flesh—Insufferable. I would fain cry out: Beware! What little sense they have is destined to dwindle away as they succumb to matrimony to men they love not, committing themselves to a lifelong servitude, without mutual respect, without decency, without— And I see the little Charlotte Lucases among them, of course: the ones convinced of their own good understanding, their preference for a quiet life, asking for nothing so much as 'a comfortable home'. They pride themselves on being above the romantic notions of their fellow creatures, while all the while, unknowingly, they are the most deluded, the most self-conceited, the unhappiest of the lot.

You deem my vision to be clouded by my own fate, Elizabeth? I protest, I have never seen clearer. What illusions of stoicism I have had have finally fallen away.

Ailsa and I have had very little time to ourselves. Stolen moments, as though we were still at Hunsford: little fingers linking together here, a walk into a dark, snowy garden there—cold iron, swift kisses, crystals melting on eyelashes.

Last night, however, we went to the opening of a play, nominally in the company of Miss Anne and Mrs J., though they were headed in the opposite direction before we had so much as reached the theatre. The play was a trifle, named after some woman or other—Isabella, I think it was. But we were glad to be on our own together, just the same; even if it had to be in a room full of strangers. Under the scant concealment of my shawl, Ailsa stroked the inside of my wrist with such a delicate touch, she fairly had me out-swooning the poor actress on stage. If only we could have taken a box.

I put up my programme before my face to hide my glowing complexion, and Ailsa bent towards me to mumble: "Can you see that woman up there, three rows to our left? No, not that one. She is wearing a white cap with a black velvet ribbon. Yes, you see her."

I studied the creature she indicated, but could find nothing out of the ordinary about her. She was of average height and build, her hair curling softly about her face, mouth small, eyes large and fine, I suppose. It was hard to make out from such a distance.

"Why? What is it you want me to observe about her?"

"Oh, Charly…" Her fingers stole up the inside of my arm, caressing the sensitive skin there, sending shivers of delight coursing through me. "Only that the lady in question is Miss A__. She is a writer, a novelist. I have it upon good authority. I thought you might like to take note of her."

I looked again, trying to catch the woman's eye. I cannot say why, but in that moment, I felt as if my life depended upon her acknowledging me. But in vain—she would not see me. As she shrewdly scanned the room, noting any acquaintances, no doubt, her gaze seemed to have glazed over by the time it alighted on me. It was as though she stared right through me: as if she could not see me at all.

"Don't fret, Lucas," my darling admonished, ever preternaturally acquainted with my private ruminations. "You'll write a story of your own some day. You needn't be in hers."

I closed my eyes and let Ailsa's stealthy caresses describe me. At the end of the second act, I turned in my seat again, but Miss A__ and her companions were gone.

Bath
January, 1816

We are in an uproar! A private uproar—it must be private—and I must write, though my hand would be illegible to anyone but my would-be confidante. My heart is likely to thump its way out of my chest. Ailsa sleeps, at last, the spasmodic, unnatural sleep that a mild sleeping potion can bestow. She has been frightened out of her wits; and so have I, on her account. Oh, that I could offer her my protection! That I could run my sword to the hilt into that demon in the flesh chasing her! That I could divest myself of the meekness of our sex for but one night, and be reborn an avenging Adrestia, a true Lucas to stand as a shield between her and that fiend, that wretch, that Beelzebub! But I am raving.

I will calm down and give you the particulars, though my heart bleeds and my soul cries out for action with every ragged breath. What can this ranting lunacy avail us? This senseless violence—yet, have I ever in my life been moved to see the justness of that most dire of penalties, surely this man...!

It is her cousin M. He is here. He has seen us. We are—she is—in mortal peril.

But has he seen us? Would he not have spirited her away on the spot, if he did see us? He could not hope for a more opportune moment—most assuredly, he could not. Out in the open, in the street, yes, but he cannot very well come calling at this house, with no pretence to her ladyship's acquaintance, with Ailsa's aversion writ large across her face. The man is a fool if he thinks he can snatch her away—unlawfully snatch her away!—while she is among her friends, even if we are an all-female party. What claim can he have on her? Her *rapist*! Oh, but I will not beat about the bush.

Today, of all days, we set out to visit the grave of Patrick and Sylvia Reid. Today of all days, I say; but what signifies the day? For all we know, that fiend has been lying in wait for her every day these three weeks past. But how was he to know we had come to Bath in the first place? Would not searching her out at her cousin Reid's have been the more obvious course of action, even if he (it! I would fain have written) could not hope to prevail upon that gentleman to give her up without resorting to arms? I shudder to envision it: mild-mannered, even-tempered Dr Reid, duelling at dawn for the ruined honour of his blighted cousin. Honour! For her life—and his, and—for my life, though he would never know it. It bears not thinking about.

But here we are, devoid of all male protection, and the coincidence... My mind shrinks from such instances of unlikely coincidences; you know me too well to doubt that, Lizzy. Ailsa insists that her Edinburgh lawyer, the only outside agent whom she has acquainted with her whereabouts, is a man of honour, of discretion—positively paternal were her words, a note of anguish in her voice that prevented further probing upon the subject. For whom can she trust? That she does not suspect me; if ever I doubted her love for me, this implicit trust in the face of adversity must convince me of its solid, unshakeable foundation. For now the earth is rent beneath our feet, and we are falling, falling...

*

Ailsa stirred, but she will not wake, I think. In her sleep, there is a deep furrow down her otherwise open and clear forehead, her brows knitted as if some physical pain tore at her from inside. The way he tore at her— But my mind must not go there. It will surely be obliterated if I dwell for too long upon it. As I wrote when I was first made acquainted with her cruel history: what good can I do her if I were locked away in an asylum for the morbidly insane?

No—today, this day, instead.

I woke up to love this morning. It boggles the mind; was it but a few hours ago that we had the leisure, the security, the imagined safety to explore and embrace each other, here in our shared bed? I woke up to love and gave love in return: my body a blissful conduit of feeling. I woke up, again and again; and when we had awoken a time too many for even our faded sense of propriety, we put on our dressing gowns and rang for chocolate. It was a beautiful day without—such an innocuous day, this day, such deceitful prettiness! We sat by the window, drinking our dishes and admiring the twinkling sun-kissed snow piling softly across streets and trees.

There was a stillness, a seriousness about this tender morning. I remember thinking as I beheld my rosy-cheeked love: she is to be my wife. I will swear my allegiance to her, my unswerving commitment to her future happiness, at her parents' grave.

I gathered her into my arms, and though neither of us spoke, there was a solemnity to that moment, which shewed me the depth of insincerity attached to my formerly having made any such vows.

Ailsa kissed me. She made that wonderful little noise against my lips, which bids me: yes. I laid her back against the seat and loved her, body, mind, and soul.

Oh, that we had never ventured out! If we could but have stayed sheltered in that pure, unadulterated joy forever.

Three hours from thence—

We had the day off from our hostesses. The ladies were gone out to call at some dowager or other who, it seems, has a son of marriageable age. Shrewdly, Lady Catherine had decided not to bring Miss Reid, for though Miss Anne's looks are uncommonly improved by her extracurricular activities here... I dare say Mrs Jenkinson will find some objection to the young man to whisper into her ladyship's ear. How at peace they were in their chosen style of life when they had Mr Fitzwilliam Darcy as a distant but tangible possibility to occupy Lady Catherine's attention. Miss de Bourgh, I am now convinced, never had any serious designs upon your husband-to-be, my Eliza. He was a mere bulwark, a convenient pet scheme of her mother's, which kept everyone's gaze averted, everyone at a loss to guess the true nature of her relationship with her governess-turned-nurse. A sickly constitution! She embraces that identity as a mask, a decoy to keep any admirers with a view of begetting heirs at bay.

I cannot but grow a tad jealous of these ladies, I admit. Not too long from hence, Miss Anne will be a wealthy and eccentric heiress, and no one will be the wiser as she firmly settles into what the world snidely refers to as old-maidenhood. What sort of visitors will be seen leaving and entering the august setting of Rosings Park then? Miss Anne de Bourgh likes to have her bottom...

But enough. I am only escaping into flights of fancy because the topic I have to write upon is too frightful for my pen not to run away on any other strain that offers itself.

Today, this day, we were to have to ourselves, and we had fixed upon it as a convenient time to visit the little abbey cemetery where the doubly unfortunate Reids had been laid to their final rest, eighteen or so years ago.

Ailsa had never been there, of course. If it had not been for Lilly's faithful account of her parents' last, desperate hours and how her uncle had declined the expense of having them (his own brother! his sister by marriage!) interred within the abbey itself—as befit their social standing—chusing instead to have them put in a remote corner of the graveyard, a single slab of marble denoting the resting place of their earthly remains, she would not have known where to look for them at all.

We took a carriage from P___ Street to the abbey, my meagre allowance from Mr C. just enough to cover such frivolities. Ailsa would have insisted on paying had she bethought herself, but my pride and her distraction would not allow it. As we approached our destination, she grew quieter and quieter, her hand continually coming up to fret at the locket she habitually wears around her neck, the one with the two faded watercolour miniatures inside: a young man and a lady with large, penetrating eyes. Frozen in time, yet unreachable, unassailable for their orphan child. Walking away from the carriage, I placed her hand at the crook of my arm, and she gave me a small, wan smile.

The grounds of the abbey are austere, yet beautifully kept, even in winter. I think we have visited this place once before, you and I, Elizabeth, in what seems to me now another life. To think that we trod along those narrow lanes while you poured the balm of steadfast friendship into my sorrow-filled bosom, my mind too depressed to countenance any companions save you and the dead surrounding us—the dead to whom my little Henry had so lately been joined. And might we not have passed by that very gravesite towards which Ailsa and I now steered our steps? Might not my eyes have flitted over those names, that inscription, my lips even forming the then meaningless syllables of Pat-rick and Syl-vi-a Reid, without it leaving any impression upon my mind, any sense of foreshadowing of what was to come?

How many times in life must we necessarily cross paths with our future selves, playing the parts of our own ghosts, and be none the wiser.

Ailsa would laugh at such <u>grave</u> reflections—laugh, and bring me out of myself.

Do not vex yourself unduly, Lucas.

Oh, but she stirs—

*

She has had a dish of tea with milk, pressed my hand, and promptly returned to her state of induced oblivion. It cannot go on like this. I must speak to Lady Catherine about cutting short our stay— But what reason shall I give?

I cannot think.

I will continue my interrupted history. We had but just come up to the marble stone, Ailsa's hand reaching out to touch it, a harrowing "Oh!" passing over her lips, when out of the corner of my eye I espied the creeping shadow of a man approaching, all clothed in sooty blacks. Creeping, I say; yet is not this an adjective I indulge in after the fact of his identity has been revealed to me? No, but there was something sinister... And yet his face—a blank—even now, I cannot...

"Ailsa," I whispered. "There is someone coming, a gentleman seems to be coming towards us. Who can it be?"

She turned her head, and for an instant I felt the full weight of her sagging against me, as if she were about to sink through the frosty ground, there and then, to join her parents in the Underworld. Instinctively, I put my arm about her, propping her up as best I could, and then her mouth was at my ear, her voice quaking with fright, a mere shadow of itself. It pierced me to my core.

"It is he! Oh, Charly, fly! We must fly. This instant!"

I could not doubt her. Her whole trembling being forbade the very notion. I blessed my oft-cursed husband for having given me the means of tipping the carriage driver handsomely enough that he lingered at the cemetery gates. Hooking my arm more firmly through Ailsa's, I hoisted up my skirts and petticoats, my woollen stockings immodestly exposed, and hurtled off. What liberty, Eliza! Even in that moment as my feet pounded the gravel path, as Ailsa ran beside me, a fresh burst of energy giving her wings, it came rushing into me: how we ran as girls, freed of the restraints of decorum, not yet old enough to have entirely been moulded to our roles as virtuous, sedate young women.

Someone called out behind us: He. Neither of us turned our heads. As we closed in on the gates I registered the shock in the coachman's eye, but took no notice of it, simply assisting—lifting—my love into the seat and shouting at him to drive on, for God's sake, man, get ye into the carriage and drive! I should have liked to say that my voice boomed, that he succumbed to my commanding air, my just wrath. But really, I believe I shrieked like a madwoman, and that surprise rather than a sense of the gravity of our situation made him heed my instructions.

That, and the rattling of the coins in my purse.

As we drove off, I finally dared to swivel in my seat and look out for our pursuer. He stood but a few feet away from the Reid tomb, his hat in hand, his fiery hair—Ailsa's hair—bright against the eerie backdrop. And I knew him, in my soul I knew him. My beloved crumpled in my arms, her bonnet askew as she curled up to my chest.

Bath
January, 1816

We must travel post. I can think of no alternative. To return to Hunsford may indeed throw the good doctor into jeopardy, but to linger in this place is unthinkable. This place: but a night ago the shimmering haven of our love. To return to the parsonage, to Mr C., willingly curtailing our stay—how loathsome it would have sounded to Charlotte of yesterday, and yet how Lucas of today burns to effect it! And will that devil incarnate pursue us? How hateful our prospects, whichever way I turn. But he must not have dared to come there, or our fate should have been decided many months ago. That he would venture to Bath— He must have an informant. There is no other explanation for it.

How grating it is that our sex is so little regarded that without a gentleman companion we are viewed as fair game. Our protection by Law is frail indeed. But two can play at this game! If I cannot fight, then at least I will do what we women are deemed to be the masters of: I will conceal.

I confess, it is all Mrs Jenkinson's idea. I have little talent for plotting, despite my love's fashioning me as an authoress. Destitute as I was of rhyme or reason, filled with despair and a vile impotency in the face of adversity, I searched out the only counsellor I could conceive of in this house. I knew she knew I knew & cetera. We are not so much sworn or bound to secrecy and affiliation as we are entangled, stuck in its web.

"Mrs Collins," she greeted me, her face inscrutable as she opened the door to her and Anne's apartment. Anne was—as I had ascertained—with her mother in the morning-room; for though I doubt not but that telling the one is tantamount to telling the other, I could not have had the courage to speak of our plight with them both before me at once. And despite everything: Anne is a de Bourgh. It is not to be thought of.

"I must speak to you in private, madam," I blurted out, before I could lose my nerve. "Ailsa is very ill. I—I must ask your advice. Forgive my forwardness, but the matter is too pressing…"

"Do not stand in the corridor, Mrs Collins," Mrs Jenkinson cut me off, placing a firm hand on my shoulder and ushering me inside. "You would do well not to start prating in the open, if you wish not to have your private affairs tattled about by the servants."

The woman clicked her tongue as she led me over to the Roman sofa in the smallish sitting-room. My face was aflame. Mrs J. sat me down with a significant smile.

"The pair of you. Such novices."

She took her seat in the chair opposite me. Her posture—her true posture, I might call it: for it occurred to me that the simpering solicitude and cowering frame she usually presents to the world and to her mistress in particular is nothing more or less than an elaborate ruse, a part she can pick up and inhabit, and slough off as easily as a door opens and closes. Her posture emanated a simmering strength, a pantheress wrapped in black damask.

"What ails your fair mistress? A lovers' spat?"

I coloured again, though I would not have thought it possible for my complexion to take on a darker hue of red than it already bore. But the convenient mirror hanging on the wall behind Mrs J. meant that I could not escape myself. I wondered if they had had it moved there purposely. I need not have wondered, though. I could tell from the half challenging, half satisfied look in Jenkinson's eye that my surmise was correct.

"It is not—we have not quarrelled. I must ask you, madam, before I begin, has Ailsa ever spoken to you of the reason she came into Kent in the first place?"

Mrs Jenkinson hesitated. Then she shook her head, a little grudgingly, I thought.

"Why no, though it is not for lack of curiosity on my part, I assure you. But she is impressively circumspect for her tender years."

I nodded and felt relief flood my tensed-up limbs. Although I had not acknowledged any conscious suspicion, I was glad to have it confirmed that the formidable ladies had not betrayed Ailsa to her cousin, all the same.

"I am afraid that I must breach her trust and share with you a little of her past life, so that you may advise me how best to help—to protect her—for I am at my wit's end. Her cousin, the cousin who is not our Dr Reid, he is here, in Bath."

Mrs J. leaned eagerly forward to hear me out. I felt a pang at the prospect of having my beloved's history bandied about by this—this strange sisterhood, as I may term it—but there was true benignity in Mrs Jenkinson's gaze, a peculiar understanding for my situation, which I could not hope to find in anyone else of my acquaintance; not even in you, my Lizzy, loath as I am to admit it.

I drew Ailsa's letter to me out of my bosom—for I always carry it with me in my escritoire—and proceeded to read out the passages pertaining to her cousin M.'s criminal treatment of her. I could not have told it in my own words or my incoherency might have put Mrs J.'s faculties of comprehension sorely to the test.

As I read, I noticed that my auditress's usually impassive features pinched with concern. Her lips thinned to a line. Her cheeks—always pale, spinster pale, as I think we have heard Colonel Fitzwilliam describe them in an unguarded moment—grew white as a newly-limed wall, making her dark, sunken eyes look the more phantom-like as they dilated with sentiment.

I hoped; I wished; I prayed that this meant she would come to our assistance in whatever way she could.

As I commenced on the affecting description of Ailsa's brush with death on the moor, Mrs Jenkinson interrupted my reading by rising to her feet, wringing her elegant hands and pacing up and down the room. Her damask rustled and shook.

"Enough! Enough, if you please, Mistress Collins. I am not used to displaying emotion in public. The man— the man, say I? The demon would be more apt. An atrocity against Nature and Reason, and yet they call *us* unnatural.

It is not to be borne. *He*, then: *he* has used her abominably, yet her tenacity in the face of such unspeakable—unhearable!—adversity shews a greatness of mind and heart that can but further exalt your dear Miss Reid to anyone who is privileged with hearing her tale. Oh, but the wretch!"

She flung again from the chair she had endeavoured to seat herself in, an active warmth animating her frame, rejecting the passive comforts of a seated position.

I could not but inwardly echo her sentiments, as all the pangs I had felt upon my first perusal of this miscreant's evil deeds came back to me, spurred by Mrs J.'s turbulent reaction. For was she not right? Must not any sensible man or woman, having the facts laid plainly before him or her, reach the same conclusion: an utter condemnation and casting-off of that foul wretch? Could we not then have recourse to the protection of a court?

"It will not do, Mrs Collins," Mrs Jenkinson warned uncannily, as if she were plucking my very thoughts out of the air and responding to them, not staying to hear them spoken aloud. "He may claim a common-law marriage to her. I hear it is the Scottish way. And besides, there is something sinister afoot. If he has had an informant divulging the lady's whereabouts, what else might this informant be privy to?"

Her dark eyes pierced mine, laying my errant soul bare and cowering under her scrutiny.

"No one," I whispered, wetting my parched lips. "Surely, no one..."

"Someone," assured me the impetuous madam, "and you must find out who it is. But first you must snatch your lady out of the maws of this threat, for who can ask that she shall have the fortitude to escape him twice? It behoves you to come to her aid, Mistress Collins, if ever you loved her."

Again I trembled beneath her shrewd stare, but, as I may say, simultaneously a fevered vehemence rose within.

"I do," I professed. "I love her most sincerely. She is dearer to me even than my own self. I would follow her to the ends of the Earth."

And is not this the truth? Why then are we not in Switzerland already, far out of reach of this grasping fiend? My cursed indecision, my reluctance to cause a scandal may have endangered her whom I would and should be ready to give up everything for. And if she had never met me, would she not be safe out of the country by now? Accompanied perchance by her brother-cousin, by her faithful Lilly, ready to take up her well-deserved life of ease, if in seclusion, after all her strife? Guilt, hopeless, crushing guilt lodged in my chest and brought fresh tears to my eyes.

Mrs Jenkinson's expression softened; she put a tentative arm about my shoulders.

"There, there," she comforted me awkwardly. "I do not doubt your earnestness, Collins. But I require you not to go to the ends of the Earth just yet. Hunsford will do, at present. And from thence..."

To Switzerland! I would have cried out, but even as it was an exquisite comfort to speak openly to another creature about our nascent plans, I knew I should hold my tongue, for Ailsa's, even for Jenkinson's own sake. The fewer who knew of our scheme the better—as our present circumstances were ample proof.

"He will pursue us. He will overtake us on the road."

Mrs Jenkinson patted my shoulder and released her hold on me.

"Not necessarily," she said and her eyes shone with a sudden enthusiasm that seemed incompatible with our dire straits. "Mrs Collins, I believe I have concocted a plan."

Eliza—I know you would not take kindly my interruption, but I must indeed stay my pen. Ailsa stirs and it is imperative that I acquaint her with the details of our planned flight. Tomorrow—

Hungerford
January, 1816

I am writing perched in a nook, my escritoire on my lap, my eyes squinting to see by the light of a single tallow. It is past midnight and the town of Hungerford appears to be at rest. I am bone-tired and eager to join them, but I know that I would regret it if I did not put down the particulars of our narrow—our far-fetched—escape while they are still fresh and shining in full splendour in my mind.

Lizzy, you would hardly know me. Except—

But you will pardon me, I must start with the scene this morning, for dramatic effect. Mrs Jenkinson, the Sisterhood, has come to our aid, effecting our exit from Bath in the deepest, most convoluted of ways. I could have thought myself drawn into one of the rake Lovelace's deceitful stratagems; but I am grateful, indebted to a degree I know not how to repay. They did it for Ailsa—as do I.

Thus, this morning, in the accommodating cloak-and-sword mist of Bath, two strange characters stole out of the back door of Lady Catherine de Bourgh's townhouse, carrying aught but one travel valise each. This was a pair unheard of by anyone in that town—or anywhere else—until the preceding night, when they had been conjured up by the machinating mind of Mrs Jenkinson. Decked in borrowed plumes, the taller of the two was sporting a gentleman's travelling habit, dapper but innocuous, the clothes not altogether an ill fit. At his side, with a pale but determined mien, was his lady apparent: hair covered by a large, brownish bonnet, with a rim that all but concealed her pretty face when she bowed her head to the ground.

The figures both glanced, one final time, up at the windows that had so recently belonged to Mrs Wm Collins and her particular friend Miss Ailsa Reid. Then, as one, they turned and hastened away.

By the time they reached the turnpike where the post chaise awaited the arrival of early-morning travellers, the sun had cleared away the last remnants of the morning mists, and their fresh and rosy features—the young man's, perhaps, in particular—seemed to belie the age-worn impression of their costumes.

The lad handed his lady and their luggage into the coach and addressed himself to the driver.

"Mr and Mrs Lucas, good man. For Hungerford."

The 'good man' was perhaps a trifle overdone. The coachman nodded curtly; then, taking in the gentlemanly appearance of his passenger-to-be, he made a half bow and gestured at the seat beside him.

"Will ye not sit by me, young Sir? It looks to be a splendid day on the road after this gloomy night and I've some warm fells here to keep us snug."

"I thank you, no. My wife has a sickly constitution and requires my attendance on her."

The man scoffed and winked.

"Don't you worry about your lady, Sir. There ain't nothing but elderly women of the lower-middling classes back there today; your madam will be amply waited upon. Trust me, you will be better off up here!"

To this young master Lucas had no reply, newly begotten as he was in the role of man and husband. He nodded, touched his hand to his hat, and sat up in the driver's box.

"Very wise, Sir," the coachman chuckled and smacked the reins to coax the horses on.

Despite the driver's cheerful loquacity, Mr Lucas kept his tongue, his face averted as if lost in meditations upon the countryside surrounding them. Although it was just above freezing in town, out on the road snow covered the ground all the way to the blue horizon, glistening in the January sunlight. Now and then, hollies and evergreens broke up the near monochrome of the landscape. A white hare with soot-tipped ears raced across a field. A dark bird of prey circled overhead. Lucas shuddered and drew the fell up closer.

"Ye ain't one of them there newfangled poets, are ye, Mr Lucas?" The coachman wiped his nose on his sleeve and spit a wad of tobacco out the side of the carriage. "Only, you're quietlike and damnably young to be married, if you'll pardon me, Sir. But I know them poets are lost in their own worlds of sensation. The sublime— isn't that what youse call it, Sir? I once had young master Shelley right here in that seat where ye're sitting with me. Newly married he was—just turned nineteen! Ye've heard of him no doubt, with that there Queen Mab? Another gentleman was carrying the book with him, and I never forget a name, me. Oh! says I, that's my friend Shelley, that is. And the gentleman obliged me by reading a great chunk of it out loud on the road to Kent. Have ye read it, Mr Lucas? Mighty fine phrases he put together."

Master Lucas shook his head, putting his hand to his hat to make sure it did not slip.

"I'm more of a Wordsworth man," he mumbled.

The coachman nodded, studying him slyly out of the corner of his eye. Lucas grasped at the first diversion he could think of.

"It so happens that I have his and Mr Coleridge's Lyrical Ballads with me wherever I go. Perhaps you would care to hear some of them? The road is long and I am afraid, as you have surmised, I am inclined by Nature to be taciturn. I have been told, however, that I have a not-unpleasant reading voice."

*

And so it came to pass that Mr Charles Lucas, on his first day in masculine attire, spent his time and voice chiefly on the recital of 'The Female Vagrant', 'Tintern Abbey' and the like, poems which, thankfully, he had learnt more or less by heart in his previous existence, for the only book he carried in his pocket was a collection of the works of John Donne. These, for private reasons, he would not read aloud, but as he had suspected from their preceding conversation—or rather, the coachman's monologue—the fellow, for all his earnest enjoyment of the poetry he heard, could not read a line himself.

"Why, you have the voice of an angel, Sir!" The man broke in at one point, overcome with feeling, and Master

Lucas's countenance flushed as prettily as any school mistress's.

At Swindon, there was a change of horses and a late afternoon repast, when Mr Lucas and his wife chose to seclude themselves with their bread and cheese and warm beer in a private room.

"Good Lord!" said his lady the moment the servant had retired, "I thought I should faint when I heard you begin to recite poetry in your normal voice!"

"Do you think he suspects me?"

Lucas tore into his meal, notwithstanding. They had neither of them had a scrap of food since the morning, hours and hours ago.

"I cannot say whether he does; I pulled up the shutter on pretence of a sudden chill. The coachman might be a dunce, but the eyebrows of the women in the coach shot up their gnarly foreheads at hearing verse lilted out in what they would have sworn on their last tooth was a female voice. I held it to be a peculiar talent of yours."

The young master groaned and struck his forehead.

"Oh! Ailsa, I'm so sorry."

The lady's expression softened, a hint of her old mirth reflected in her eyes. She bent forward and let her finger stroke the tender spot between the thumb and forefinger of Lucas's left hand.

"Well, it is," she murmured, her sweet smile making her husband's heart leap within his chest. "Just one of your many talents, Lucas."

*

They arrived at Hungerford well after dark, the last but two travellers to leave the coach. The driver saluted his cotton-mouthed friend Lucas, telling him he should not be surprised if he learnt that he had made a name for himself on the stage.

Lucas put his hand to his hat and offered his arm to his wife, as they made their way to the inn opposite the newly rebuilt parish church.

"We have naught but the attic room available, Sir, I beg your pardon."

"The attic will suit us fine, thank you."

The innkeeper looked from the audacious wife to the wan husband, who managed a faint smile and a shrug of his shoulder.

"The lady has spoken, I think."

He had to turn his head away at that, to avoid shewing the grimace that passed over his features as the lady in question, very quietly, stepped on his toes.

"Well, if you're sure..." The innkeeper's voice wavered.

"We're very sure. Anything will be more comfortable than the stables, will it not?"

"The stables! Upon my word!"

Ailsa triumphed. "And those were good enough for the Lord, our Saviour, after all."

The innkeeper threw up his hands, admitting defeat. "The lady drives a shrewd argument, good Sir."

"Oh, yes," the young master agreed, winking at his wife as if they shared some private jest. "She is the crown of her sex."

*

And thus we have kept up the charade throughout the course of this phantasmagorical day, until at long last we reached the privacy of our own chamber, under the roof ridge of the Golden Hare.

"Oh, Lucas."

Ailsa fell upon me the moment we had fastened the door, knocking the tall hat clean off my head. She dug her fingers greedily into my hair and began to pull out the hairpins we had used to keep my unmanly tresses in check. As they fell free, strand by strand, she sighed, and I could not forbear smiling at the ambiguous figure I must strike, with a woman's hair and face atop a slender, smart-looking gentleman's body.

"You have never been more beautiful to me."

My unease must have shewn, for she hastened to add: "Not as a man, Charly. I simply meant that you have been concealed from me all day, and now I can unwrap you like a precious gift—*my* precious gift—and no one in the world knows what treasures have been hidden underneath that foppish exterior."

So saying, she made me shrug off the greatcoat Mrs J. had obtained for me from one of the Sisters, who, it would seem, has a habit of going about dressed as a man. Ailsa untied my cravat and burrowed her nose at the nape of my neck.

"So many layers," she mumbled. "I cannot see why ladies are accused of wearing an overabundance of layers, when here you are as a man, clothed in just as many! I shall fall asleep before I have you fully undressed."

I laughed and glanced over at the narrow cot.

"Perhaps we should sleep. It's been a long day's journeying and tomorrow will be just as fatiguing."

"Perhaps," she agreed. "But first I need to make certain that you are indeed who you say you are, Master Lucas. All day I have sat in that coach, burning to get my hands on you."

She put her hand to my breeches, and I gasped as I felt the heel of it press against my tenderest parts. The familiar throb came as an instant response to her touch. A flutter of anticipation swept through me.

"Not so many layers here," she cooed and began to unbutton the front flap, her mouth busy placing little kisses up my neck and along my jaw.

I was powerless to resist her gentle but insistent advances, even had I wished to do so.

I did not. After all the upheavals of the last two days, after our real and counterfeit escape—for even as Mr and Mrs Charles Lucas snuck out the back door, trusty Hannah would have found a letter in the apartment belonging to Mrs Collins and Miss Reid, addressed to Lady Catherine de Bourgh, wherein it was intimated that an urgent message from Dr Reid had bid us return to Hunsford without delay, on the next available express—after all this, I say, I could not imagine anything sweeter than to touch and be touched in return.

I craved it—craved her—with all my heart.

"Ailsa," I whispered, her name a charm, a password to a realm of our own. "Ailsa."

She pressed into me, her lips searching mine. The front flap of my borrowed breeches fell open. I leant back against the door, my hands clutched in her skirts, and she was inside me, physically as well as mentally, stirring my very soul.

*

I wish you could know her, Lizzy. This extraordinary being, who has made a virtue of what would commonly be called vice. Who has brandished me with the mark of her affection and set my heart, the heart I thought had been buried with little Henry at the rectory of Hunsford, passionately aflame.

Once before, only, have I burnt like this. I cannot—I will not—pass it over twice.

*

Tomorrow we are bound for Newbury and from thence to Basingstoke. In a day or so, at the most, we shall be back at Hunsford. And from thence...

Basingstoke
February, 1816

Colder today, brisker; a churlish driver and but a few fellow passengers. I have sat in the coach with Ailsa, her head lolling against my shoulder, as the empty winter landscape passed by outside. A dark foreboding—but I must banish such maudlin thoughts from my stupefied mind! Ailsa reads my face like an open book, and she grows quieter, brooding.

Our only hope is that cousin M. is busy chasing spectres of his own: the post for Kent by the direct route, two ladies travelling unaccompanied by any man.

Can we trust Mrs Jenkinson, the Sisterhood, to keep our secrets? The lure of a rich reward will not tempt Mrs J.—unless she has a clandestine yearning for independence, which... I think not. Little as I can pretend to understand the dynamics of her relationship to Miss Anne de Bourgh, I rather suspect that dependence is somehow intrinsic to it.

But as for what she may let slip to the other Sisters, what they, in turn, may feel occasioned to hint...

I must sleep. Another day will see us at Hunsford, where I shall creep into the woods like a thief and change back into my title role as Mrs Collins.

How strange that this role, which is lawfully mine, should feel so much more like deceit than the part of Mr Charles Lucas, a chimaerical, utterly fictitious character.

Hunsford Parsonage
February, 1816

My dearest Eliza,

We are come home, but to what misery! It now appears our departure from Bath coincided within but a few hours with the arrival of a very real missive from Dr Reid, urging us to return by whichever means necessary.

And why? You may well ask why. The household at the village is in disarray; Lilly—my love's preserver from such a tender age, her saviour from that Hell upon the moors—has caught the symptoms of the ague.

Ailsa is beside herself. Dr Reid is grave and quiet. Cousin M.—quite forgotten.

Although Lady Catherine will hardly approve of our rushing off to attend the deathbed of a servant, it offers but too convenient an explanation for our actions. Though at what cost! My heart bleeds for Ailsa: to lose her soul's mother, if not that of her flesh, so hard upon the renewed threat to her person. Is this our punishment?

Dear God. Dear Lord Almighty. Dearest, loveliest Elizabeth. I am wringing my hands, the ink from my quill staining the sleeves of my frock. It will not do; my husband must excuse me; I must go to her presently. I fear that her spirit might not sustain this final, additional blow. I fear that her heart might break beyond repair. I fear—Oh!—but that she will catch the infection, and if she does, she shall not be the only victim!

*

Night. I am back from the doctor's. The light has gone out.

*

Early morning. Sleep eludes me. Daybreak is an hour away, but I must write: I cannot abide this tossing and turning in my solitary bed. William is at home, in his own rooms; I have hardly spoken to him since our dramatic return. He is concerned—not for me, not for Lilly, not for the doctor, nor Ailsa, no—he is concerned for the effect our rude retreat might have had on that lady who is ever foremost in his thoughts. I cannot speak to him! I have no patience, Lizzy; I fear that I used up all that noble, meek, self-effacing patience too early in life. But I am weary. I am weary to the very marrow, and that produces more or less the same result.

Last night, after my husband had said the final prayers over the unfortunate at Dr Reid's, I stole away to the woods and buried the costume of Mr Charles Lucas as deep as I could in the hard, unyielding ground. And I wept. I wished—God forgive me, but I wished I had never laid eyes on Miss Ailsa Reid.

Or rather, I wished that she might never have laid eyes on me.

For now I know how impossible—these vain, broken dreams—the world!

I must take my refuge to the narrative mode, if only to quieten my frayed and torn nerves.

I went back to the doctor's yesterday to wait upon Ailsa, first and foremost: to shew her that nothing, not even death or lethal infection, could keep me away. I was admitted by James and waited in the parlour for a quarter of an hour, pacing the room like a forlorn moth who has been lured indoors by candlelight and cannot, for the life of him, find his way out again.

When at last she came to me, she fell about my neck, and I held her, rocking her like once I rocked the slender remains of my inanimate child.

"Charly, Charly," she repeated. "Good God."

"How soon, Ailsa?"

"Tom says she will not last the night. We arrived in the nick of time. I cannot bear it! She looks upon me as if she never knew me! She raves—"

I sat us down on the sofa, gathering her again into my arms. Where she belonged, I thought. Where she must be.

"What does she say?"

"Oh! nothing intelligible. Blood and bairns and heresy. She is in agony, she blames herself; she is not the Lilly I knew. It is as though..."

She hid her face at my bosom, as if she would fain hide herself from the world. I stroked her quavering back and tucked in a curl that had escaped from the simple twist she had gathered her hair into. No Lilly to help her. Never more.

"As though?" I inquired gently and her arms tightened around me. But before she could speak, the door opened and Dr Reid entered, bowing and excusing himself, humming and hawing.

"Tom!" Ailsa sprang up. "What is it? Why would you leave her side? Oh, please God, don't tell me!"

"Hush now, cousin. Pray, strive to compose yourself. Lilly is sleeping. I have given her something for the pain. I came down to ask Mrs Collins's leave to entrust you in her care while I set out to fetch her husband. It is time, Ailsa. You must prepare yourself."

He looked at me, and I nodded my mute assent. I struggled to gain sufficient mastery over my voice to speak. I swallowed and coughed and, finally, as Dr Reid was turning to leave the room I managed: "Sir, if you please. I am afraid my husband has gone to the Netheringstead farm. Old Mr Randall is..."

My voice gave way anew. I could not pronounce the word in my fair inconsolable's presence. The doctor dipped his head. He took my meaning.

As soon as we were on our own again, Ailsa turned to me and took my hand in hers. She was pale with grief.

"Charly..."

"I understand. I will come with you."

With a small—a very small indeed—smile of gratitude, she threaded her arm through mine, the yellow muslin of her gown swishing against my muted greys. I did not need to ask; I know my love well enough by now to guess that she wore her crisp summer attire in manifest protest against the lugubrious shades of mourning. She would not resign herself to the funereal knoll until the last breath had been drawn. There is something invincible, and terrible, and wonderful in this unbending will of hers. This unbending Life.

We went around to the back stairs and walked up the rickety spiral staircase to the servants' quarters.

"I wanted to move her," Ailsa whispered, her voice distant, veiled. "I wanted to move her to the room next to my own, but she would have none of it."

Of course not, I thought, though I simply squeezed her arm. For all her boisterous, less-than-servile ways, Lilly was not in fact one for tearing down the outward structures of social class and rank. And she had that stubbornness unto death: the one that had kept the pair of them alive through everything. That illness should strike now; it was too cruel a blow on the side of Fate.

"Do you know—does Dr Reid know what disease it is that has gripped her?"

Ailsa shook her head.

"The symptoms, in a medical sense, are vague and inconclusive. At first she suffered from vomiting and convulsions. Her stomach pains her and her hair—Oh, Charly!—her hair is coming loose. It is as if she is falling to pieces before my very eyes, my touch aggravating rather than alleviating her strife. I have never felt so powerless, so wretchedly helpless; no, not even when—"

I put my arm about her shaking shoulders, and she stopped, at the top of the stairs, allowing herself to be held a moment longer.

"I wish I could tell her," she muttered against my neck, her warm breath tickling the fine hairs of my skin. "I wish I could say she needn't be anxious on my account, for I have found my life's companion and whatever happens..."

"I will stand by you," I finished her sentence. "Come what may."

A loud, harrowing groan of pain interrupted us and hastened our feet to the door of a small chamber, little more than a garret, at the end of the dark corridor. As Ailsa pulled it open, I had to put my kerchief to my nose and mouth, for the stench, I am infinitely sorry to say, was abysmal. Little Nelly Smith from the grocer's, who has been Dr Reid's scullery maid since last year, hurried out with a chamber pot as we entered, the contents of which beggars description. She was flushed and cowed, poor girl—worried, no doubt, that she would catch whatever it was that had felled the vivacious Lilly within the span of a few days.

The cramped space within was sepulchral, lit by a single candle by the side of the bed. Under a mass of blankets and sheets, some brought—I recognised with the ghost of a blush crossing my face—from the mistress's own bedchamber, something stirred. Something, I say, for the unhappy wretch looked nothing like the impetuous Lilly we had left behind less than two months ago.

Ailsa flew to her side, fell to her knees and put her head on the side of the pillow like a little girl might do; like she had done, I doubt not, in that orphaned childhood of hers, when she knew of no other mother than this doting, kind-hearted servant.

I looked about me and found a stool by the foot of the bed.

"My darling," Lilly rasped, a claw-like hand coming out from under the covers to place itself on Ailsa's fair head. "My precious gem. You came back to your poor Lilly—a miracle, such a miracle..."

She coughed and drew a sharp breath.

"Who is that with you, child? My eyesight is failing me. Who is there, pray? Is it your cousin?"

"It is Char... It is Mrs Collins, dear."

Ailsa would have said more; I could see it in the glassy brightness of her eyes, on her trembling lips, but Lilly let out an unearthly howl which turned, by and by, into a harsh, blood-stained cough. Silent tears fell down my beloved's cheeks, even as she calmly, steadily, drew her kerchief from her bosom and used it to wipe the dew of sweat and blood from Lilly's face.

I looked at my hands, folded uselessly in my lap. I am sorry to say that I have never possessed that natural womanly talent for allaying the fears and abetting the comforts of the sick and dying. I know not what to say or do. But I was there for Ailsa, and I could but hope that my presence, in some measure, did her good.

As for Lilly, I was not so sure. Thus, you may imagine my consternation when the wizened woman tried to sit up against the pillows behind her, and her cloudy gaze seemed to search mine.

"My dove," she breathed. "Ailsa, dear, do be an angel and fetch me a dish of tea. I should not ask it of you—indeed, I should not—only that I doubt that Nelly will be on her way back here anytime soon. Will you play the servant to your old friend, my beloved Miss Reid? Daughter of my heart, more dear to me than any kin, living or dead?"

"Oh, Lilly, I would fetch you the moon! You know I would. If only..."

"Come, child. What would I do with the moon?"

A glint of humour passed over her bedraggled features, a last gasp, as it were, of the old Lilly. She put her palm to Ailsa's cheek.

"Go, love. Only for a minute or two. I need to speak to your friend."

Ailsa's eyes brimmed; her chest rose as if she took a breath to speak, then it fell again in a sigh. She gave us both a trepidatious smile and stood to leave the clogged air of the sickroom. As she passed me, her hand touched my shoulder.

"I will be back presently."

I bowed my head. The wishes of the dying must be fulfilled if at all possible; even if I would have much preferred, would have found it only natural and right that I rather than Ailsa should have been asked to leave on the pretence of hunting for a dish of tea. The abject nobility of death is not to be questioned, though in hindsight: dear God!

"Come closer, Mistress Collins. Draw your seat up, if you please. Do not trouble yourself: I am not contagious."

Lilly's hand beckoned to me; her head had fallen back, spent with exertion. Her assertion seemed dubious, but I would not quibble with it. I brought the stool over to where Ailsa had bent her knee a moment ago.

"She is the light of my life," the older woman murmured, and there was something about her grim expression, the mask of unspeakable agony that had been moulded onto her once so gay features, which chilled the very blood in me. "Even now, it infinitely gladdens my heart to see her, to have her at my side in this last hour, and yet..."

Her milky eyes caught mine, and I started. There was menace in them, a hatred so profound that my soul shrank from its intensity. My hand came up to my chest, and I drew back.

"No, you shall not go, Mrs Collins. You shall hear me out, and you shall assist me, or by all that is good and holy, my restless soul shall haunt yours for an eternity. Look at me, woman—fiend—hermaphrodite, whatever you are."

My head throbbed in a way I had been spared, I realised, for a full month. Not even in the nightmare of our last days in Bath had I succumbed to its siren call of pain. Now, I welcomed the distraction. I pressed my fingers to my temple and met the madwoman's gaze.

"It was for her sake," she complained, and an odd note of petulance had crept into her voice that jarred with the gravity of her deathbed confession. "It was all for her. I pulled her out of the very jaws of the Devil, only to find that he would not admit defeat—no, not he!—but would clothe himself in the unlikeliest of habits, would make himself a She-devil to complete her ruin! Yes, Mrs Collins, I see your mind at work. It was I who communicated your whereabouts to my lady's cousin, and I would do so again. He may spell the end of her mortal coil—but you! You would threaten her immortal soul!"

She broke off, racked by a coughing fit. I sat frozen in place. I could not make sense of the information she had given me, even as it seemed to grate at my being, drag the most precious thing I had in life through the mud.

"Open the drawer to your left, if you please. There's a vial..."

Dazed, I did as I was told. Amid a motley collection of a poor woman's treasures—strings, pieces of cloth, a pair of scissors—was, indeed, a glass vial, of a greenish tint, half filled with a white powder. I lifted it up.

"I would not have Master Reid find it. He is too astute a man, though a useless protector of his saintly cousin. If things had gone according to plan, if she had been on her way back to Scotland by now, then it would not have mattered. It would have been to my credit."

"You... You've poisoned yourself?" There was a din at my ears. Lilly leaned towards me, and I recoiled, but not swiftly enough; she snatched the vial out of my hands, uncorked it and emptied its contents into her mouth. She gaped like a baby bird, then licked her lips.

"Take it with you." She thrust the empty vial back into my hands. "And do not let me have died in vain, Mistress Collins. If ever there was a woman residing in that unnatural flesh of yours, if you are not consummately in allegiance with the Dark One: leave her be. Will you promise me? Gladly will I purchase her immortality at the expense of my own. Oh, gladly..."

Her eyes rolled up into her head. The door creaked. Hastily, unthinkingly, I slipped the vial into the pocket of my heavy woollen gown.

"Lilly!"

There was a clatter as Ailsa put the tea tray on a chest of drawers and dashed towards us, a despairing, unhinged look on her. I bowed over the still creature in the bed and shook my head.

"She is asleep. I fear—I fear she will not wake up."

"Oh, Lilly! Oh, mother, mother..."

A shudder went through me as Ailsa fell prostrate at the side of the bed, weeping bitterly.

"Why did she send me away? Why? What did she tell you?"

"I..." The pang of pain at the left side of my face forced me to sink back onto the stool. I looked at the shrivelled shape of the woman who had been the means of saving this innocent from the depths of human misery on Earth, yet would have thrown her back into it again to keep her— from me.

Ailsa lifted her head. I felt as though someone had blown out the last burning candle in me. All was darkness. All was dead.

"She told me she loved you."

*

I cannot say when I shall write again, Eliza. If ever I may.

Volume Three

Hunsford
March, 1816

Dearest Elizabeth,

A full month has passed since last I set pen to paper to write to this invented version of you, who at times—to my infinite discredit—I find to be more real, more animated in my mind than the contented, friendly yet distant mother of two, alive and well at Pemberley.

There are times when I think if I had never known you... But how vain are such thoughts. Who can say when the poison ran into my veins, when it took hold, when it firmly settled into the very make-up of this God's forsaken creature, this She-devil walking the Earth in the guise of a rector's wife?

In my hand as I write this, I turn the vial that Lilly thrust upon me in the hour of her parting. There is not a smidgen of the contents left; she cleared away the evidence and went, satisfied to be a lost soul, to sacrifice herself only to wring from me that promise which has sealed my fate.

I have lost my way. I go through my days in a haze of pain, eating very little, speaking even less, attending to my poultry and visiting the village poor. At first, messages came in the morning, respectfully requesting my presence at the doctor's. I sent my excuses; I sent my husband; I sent Travis with her lamb stew. I did not go to the service where Lilly's earthly remains were committed to their final resting place. If people had known what I know, she should have been buried at the crossroads.

As should I.

William has come to my bed on the odd Saturday night, and I—I have let him. My body is not my own. I contracted it away, and I must resign myself. If only I had done so before, how much misery should I have spared *her*, whose very name my pen aches to write. I—

I have collected myself. Spring is upon us; the green buds are pushing at their confinements, and I will go out, I think, to join my woe to theirs.

I have been told that she is preparing for her departure. She has not been accompanying Dr Reid to Lady Catherine's dinner parties. She is in mourning, says he, gently but firmly, and he will not let himself be swayed by her ladyship's impertinent commands to bring the girl out of these unseemly notions of repining the loss of a servant.

Mrs Jenkinson has tried to catch me on my own, but I have remained chained to my husband's side. There is an increasing look of disgust on her features when she turns her gaze on me. She has been to call at the doctor's, as Lady Catherine could not forbear mentioning, and I shudder to think what A—what must have been said about me.

I am to blame. I am forever to blame. There is nothing I can do now—but I will go out. I should not have picked up my writing again. The ink flows too willingly under my hand, seducing me into thoughts of what I must not think of, luring me away from my resolutions, away from those obligations which it is in no mortal's power to defray.

Adieu.

*

Night. Oh, but my soul bleeds!

Hunsford
April, 1816

This morning, there was a rose on the grave of my little Henry, and I fell to my knees as though I had been struck from behind. Had she written me a letter full of recriminations, had she accosted me at church, come to Lady Catherine's—all, all I could have born, but this. This simple gesture which brought home the full force of that gentle, forgiving, all-encompassing love that I am obliged to give up, crushing me to the ground. Alas, there is not much left to crush.

I took the rose and brought it to my lips, tenderly kissing each petal, as silent tears rained down my cheeks. I whispered her name to it. I buried my nose in it as I would have buried it at her neck, in that instant, had she been present, and I thought: I shall not be safe until she has gone. *She* shall not be safe from me.

I do not know how long I tarried, the damp of the grass suffusing my coat and gown, the wind drying my tears even as new ones formed, until I could weep no more. Spring has brought death, as the cold winter saw the bloom of our love. We are out of season.

After returning the rose to where it had lain, I took out my handkerchief to wipe the salty stains from my face. But a gust of wind caught it, and it flew out of my hand: a strange, spectral butterfly of untold grief.

I was too weary to chase after it. I turned and trod back home.

*

I rest in her arms at night. She visits my dreams, giving me no respite, no blessed forgetfulness. But tonight I dreamt of my wedding, at the simple country church in Hertfordshire, and as I was about to give my vows in response to William's, you rose from your seat and came up to us, Eliza, and said, very quietly yet adamantly: *No.*

*

Ailsa, Ailsa, Ailsa...

*

Morning. We have had a letter from Meryton, and we must make haste. There is not a moment to lose; oh, beloved sister! I must pack up my writing desk.

Bromley
April, 1816

We are changing horses, and there is not much time to write; I have begged off a meal at the Bell. I cannot eat. My head aches in such a way I feel as though my eyes should bleed, but nothing comes.

Dr Reid is being very attentive, if, as is natural, distracted. My thoughts are all in disorder.

Maria is gravely ill. Mamma fears consumption, the pox— She does not know what she fears. The apothecary, Mr Shirley, has told her we must prepare ourselves for the worst. The boys are at school, which is a mercy; the rest of the household are confined from society at large. She writes that we mustn't come, but that is impossible to contemplate.

My husband—the odious little man!—has stayed behind, shirking his familial duties, out of fear, folly, weakness. Well! Her ladyship will keep him busy penning nonsense to my father, no doubt.

And so, am I unattended? You see I am not; Dr Reid, whom Destiny guided to our doorstep on the morning I received the blighted news, can think of no other patient, can think of nothing but carrying me to my sister's side in order to offer his second opinion. And whither he goes, his cousin must follow—for as long as she remains in this country under his protection. Oh! Lizzy, no one knows better than I the danger of leaving her behind at Hunsford. But to be thrown so suddenly into her immediate presence, to have all her kind solicitude, her earnest compunction at Maria's illness, the comfort of her voice in my ears as she speaks to me and Tom by turns. She utters little nothings, commonplaces; and yet the balm of her words sustains our spirits, offers a small but constant beacon of light through our gloom.

Already, I have reached for her hand twice, recollecting myself only at the very last. How many miles yet?

I am told that our chaise is in readiness. Presently then—

Lucas Lodge
April, 1816

Elizabeth,

I am in my old apartment at the Lodge, and without Mr Collins by my side, the servants are struggling not to refer to me as Miss Lucas. I do not mind in the least; only that the title has been Maria's these four years, and I would not have them forget her.

Her fever is greatly alarming, though Dr Reid, godsend that he is, says we should take comfort: it is a good sign. Only in his patients who have outlived this malady has he observed a like progression. He will not, however, be prevailed upon to quit the sickroom. He sleeps, in fits and starts, continually at the ready, in a large armchair at the foot of her bed. Poor Mr Shirley finds himself quite unemployed.

Mamma misses your mother's company dreadfully, I dare say. She writes to Longbourn by the hour, receiving detailed accounts of the effect of my sister's disorder upon Mrs Bennet's nerves, injudiciously interspersed with exultant descriptions of her growing number of grandchildren.

Who can account for this friendship founded upon mutual conceit and self-importance? Neither of us have ever understood the inner workings of our mothers. Perhaps, indeed, this is not the time to question any relief Lady Lucas imagines she might derive from reading Mrs

Bennet's frequent missives. Here I sit, after all, writing to my own artificial comforter fashioned in the likeness of that lady's secondborn.

Papa is glad of our arrival, and glad of Dr Reid's appearance in particular. Tom's word is now the Law with him. His distress at Maria's life-threatening condition is real and profound; she was ever a favourite with him, as you know. By rights, I should say she was ever a favourite with everyone, for though she has not your sister Jane's wisdom, nor handsomeness, in health she possesses a bright-eyed prettiness and all her sweet-tempered good nature. Such a treasure to us all! For her, indeed— But I should not even be thinking about— I must prepare for our evening repast.

*

Night. How strange it is to wander through the corridors of this my birthplace, my childhood home, as if I were haunting my own past. Lucas Lodge is quieter than I have ever known it to be, as though the house itself, with bated breath, awaited the outcome of this its most recent calamity. The floorboards creak and groan with each step I take, methinks— This is an illusion, to be sure: my distraught mind conjuring omens out of the innocuous. I can find no rest.

The greater part of the day I sit by my sister's prostrate form, wringing my hands in my utter powerlessness to stay the harrowing effects of her infection. A fine dew of sweat sits perpetually upon her brow, her fingers tracing illegible figures over the bedding that covers her. She is insensible to the world around her, to the muffled voices that come and go, to Ailsa's softly whispered words of comfort in her cousin's ear, to said cousin's regular observations of her pulse and temperature.

I could have wept as I beheld the drawn looks on my parents' faces at our evening meal tonight, as my eyes fell on the conspicuously vacant seats of Maria and Dr Reid. No doubt, we would have been eating in silence, if at all, if it hadn't been for Ailsa describing the fulsome impression Maria had made on everyone on her visit to Kent this autumn, how she cannot but expect that such a foundation of naturally youthful vigour must prevail in the face of any acute ailment. Little by little, she endeavoured and succeeded to make Papa and Mamma tell their own stories of illnesses endured and conquered, dexterously steering them away from thoughts of siblings lost, children succumbed.

Even I, who see what she is about, cannot help but be momentarily cheered by the number of instances of miraculous revivals we have amassed together.

After such intolerable blows as life has allotted her, that *I*—that she can rise again to the task of comforting others...

Lizzy, it is incredible. She is incredible. If there was any way I could—

But then, Maria's wretched form comes before my mind's eye, her pallid demeanour, her damp and matted hair clinging to her temples, her throat, her lips dry and chapped, her eyes unfocused as if already lost to this world. How can I even ponder acquitting myself!

Not that I suspect my sister's fatal condition to be due to any supernatural retribution for my former actions; I have not quite suspended my powers of reason as far as that. But Maria, dearest, loveliest, how shall we ever...? How cruel a fate that you rather than I—you who would carry our parents through any ordeal, who would never fall short or disappoint, never waver, while I...

*

Morning. I can hardly make out what I wrote last night. I am racked by guilt, turned in upon myself with worry—the mental strain—Stay. Someone is at the door.

Lucas Lodge
April, 1816

It was Ailsa at the door, and I had all but fainted; the solemnity of her features led me to believe she was bringing bad tidings. My hand reached for her arm, quite of its own, and she started, but then she smiled; and it was the spring sun breaking through months and months of rain, Eliza—it was as if—in that moment—

"She is out of danger, Charly. Her fever has broken."

I burst into tears. Ailsa wrapped me up in her arms, her heart pounding against my chest, as if it would fain have leapt from one to the other. My tears flowed over the shoulder of her gown, into her hair; I put my nose to her hairline and inhaled deeply. She smelled of the sick chamber, of sadness, of perspiration. And she smelled, exquisitely, of herself.

Breaking away from me, she pulled a handkerchief from her bosom to dab at my face. It retained the warmth of her, and I leaned into it, hungrily.

Shakily, she smiled anew, and this time I saw the depths of my own longing reflected in the glow of her eyes. I reached for her.

"Do not kiss me, Lucas." Her voice was low and rough around the edges, filled with an invitation that belied her words. "For if you do, I shan't be able to stop myself, and we must go and tell your papa and mamma. I promised

Tom we would, and she is stirring, Charly—she is really coming to!"

"Oh, Ailsa…" I started to laugh and nodded, dazed with a giddy, breathtaking species of joy. I folded up the handkerchief and presented it back to my Redeeming Angel, but she shook her head, hooking her arm through mine and leading me down the hallway and stairs towards my mother's morning-parlour.

"You might need it yet," she whispered. "And besides, it's yours."

I looked down at the piece of cloth in my hand, even as we were knocking on the parlour door, awaiting admission. It was, indeed, an old handkerchief of my own, the last one I had since before my marriage, monogrammed with an embroidered CL. I thought I had lost it, that day at the churchyard, by Henry's grave. I glanced queryingly at Ailsa.

"I caught it," she said simply, and then the door was opening and all was happiness and weeping and Maria

Lucas Lodge
1st of May, 1816

Maria is improving by the hour. The first languor of her returning health got over, she is now as sprightly and rosy-cheeked as ever you saw her, Lizzy. Your kind letter, shrewdly directed to me here at the Lodge, was a welcome reminder that your own dear self, the flesh and blood Elizabeth of the present hour, has not entirely forgotten the ways of her old friend Charlotte. I answered it with a warm cordiality which may perchance surprise you, but I hope you will attribute it to the state of emotional upheaval which naturally occurs after a fright like the one given to us all by Maria's distemper.

To be perfectly frank, I forgot myself. I had to cross out and blot the beginnings of an account of Ailsa, which I will indulge in here by and by. I see now the dangers of keeping a double ledger.

Maria was glad to see us all, was all gratitude and solicitousness; but never did her eyes shine brighter or her cheeks glow with something more than mere filial affinity than when she turned them on her dear physician-in-waiting. Poor Mr Shirley again, I say: quite forgot! Though to be fair, he chimed the death knoll a while too early for such a young and tenacious creature.

Dr Reid has now the leisure to leave the room whenever someone else is attending his patient, and his own appearance is greatly improved by it. He has had some sleep and a bath, and is positively radiant with love. I believe Mamma would have thought the match an inferior one, had he not swept in at such a crucial point in time and saved, in a manner of speaking, us all. Now the man can do no wrong, and the profession of the medical man is surely the most noble; infinitely to be preferred to the Army or Navy, at any rate. She cannot think why an Admiral should be in line for a baronetcy, when a physician's services are of so much more vital use to the kingdom.

"Excellent," says Papa. "A capital notion, my dear."

They are silly creatures, Lizzy, but I love them dearly.

And speaking of the tenderer feelings, I promised myself I would let my ink run once more on that strain which ever, despite my efforts to remove it, lies closest to my heart. Miss Ailsa Reid. Miss Reid. Ailsa. Even writing her name sends a thrill through my veins.

Impossible! Impossible that she should forgive my desertion of her in her time of need. Impossible that I should allow myself to be forgiven. Impossible that Lilly… Oh, I shall never be able to tell my love the full, atrocious extent to which her soul's mother turned on her. I cannot, even at this point, write about it with equanimity, think on it without finding myself hopelessly entangled in a web of grief and guilt. But my darling has reminded me not to confuse God's judgement with that of Man's. In her charming, easy way, she has released me, at least in part, from the agonies of self-recrimination.

It should not be possible. And yet I assure you, Elizabeth, she has taught me to hope, where all hope should have been lost.

I dropped my handkerchief. She picked it up, and then she proceeded to kiss the tears from my cheeks, until I was crying as much from joy as from sorrow.

But let me revert to the chronological order of events. After all the first jubilant felicitations on Maria's budding recovery had ended, Mamma withdrew to give Mrs B. the happy news at once. My father took it upon himself to write to the boys, forgetting that this would be the first they heard of the matter. Still, they will be glad to receive a letter from their papa, I think, all the same. I was loath to leave my sister's bedside, I own, but her strength was fading fast with her efforts to keep her eyes open on my account. I pressed my lips to her cooling temple and told her she could send for me with but a moment's notice, and at all events, I would certainly be back to read to her later in the day.

"Oh, Lotty, I'm glad," she breathed, half lost to sleep already. "You have such a good reading voice. I always thought so."

My eyes could not fail to meet Ailsa's across the room, and her small, secret smile confirmed that she too was brought to think of the last time my—or should I say, Mr Charles Lucas's—reading voice had been praised. My confusion must have been all but tangible.

Fortunately, Maria's eyelids had fluttered to a close, her breathing calm and even.

Ailsa opened the door very quietly, and I hastened to join her. I would not lose her company just yet. I could not.

As we came into the corridor, her eyes fell on the large bay window that looks out onto the lawn. The first of May sunshine was resplendent, falling in soft, warm swathes through the glass.

"Mrs Collins," said she, and I was startled by her formality, before I remembered the maidservant Mary sitting just inside the door, having made a faithful promise to Dr Reid not to stir from her lady's side until he returned from his much-needed repose. "There seems to be a little grove of alders surrounding a pond on the far edge of the garden. I should like to take a turn there, if you would favour me with your company."

Her eyes met mine as she spoke, glittering in a way that gainsaid the stilted formality of her speech. My chest swelled. I drew her arm through mine.

"I am at your disposal, Miss Reid."

*

Having fetched our coats and bonnets, we set out across the lawn, the fresh blades of grass crunching beneath our feet. It was a glorious day. The sun itself seemed to rejoice at Maria's reprieve. I felt a sting of envy at the golden path that lay before her and our eminent physician. But I could not, indeed, be jealous of her. Even if she were not my sister, there is something about her genial disposition that seems to entitle her to a fair and easy life. Maria cannot fail to be contented.

And I could not but be happy, there and then, leading the love of my life through the grounds of Lucas Lodge, listening to her little cries of rapture at my childhood's delights. Our childhood's, I should say, Lizzy. I would never have thought I should have the chance to shew her this.

As we approached the alders, we both of us fell silent. The water in the pond lapped against the shore in the temperate breeze. A single, bright yellow lily swelled at its centre. My pulse raced. My breathing came in short, rapid intakes. Ailsa heard it and pressed her arm closer to my side, her hip brushing mine through our coats and frocks. She led me up to the trunk of an alder tree leaning out across the water, out of view from the main building. There, she took me in her arms, as though I had been out of them for but a few hours rather than an excruciating two months. I trembled, enthralled, as she pressed my back up against the tree.

"You will not deny me this, Charly," she mumbled, and the depth of raw yearning in her eyes left me in no doubts as to her intentions.

It was as though the sun had burnt its way into me. I shook my head vehemently. The relief of the last few hours had left me ripe and aching for another kind of release. I wanted her badly. Her taste, her scent, her hand in mine, her lips at my collarbone, her teeth digging into my flesh as I brought her to the *pointe de crise* among the squeaky green lily-of-the-valley leaves surrounding us.

But first I must let her claim what was rightfully hers. Her need could brook no opposition. I must allow her to take the lead.

She untied and removed her bonnet, casting it aside with an impatience that brought fresh heat to my countenance. I stood quite still. She fell to her knees in front of me, among the May Day greenery, and I thought she would get stains on the skirt of her mourning weeds; it was imprudent; and then I could think no more, as she lifted the hems of my frock and undergown and disappeared from view altogether.

Her breath was hot and humid, tickling my skin even through the thinly worn cotton of my underthings. I braced myself against the alder, my hand clapped over my mouth as her fingers and tongue began their sweet work on me, teasing the cotton this way and that. My legs shook. I listed against the listing tree trunk, her mouth growing fervent, her hands clasping my trembling thighs.

She nipped at my swollen flesh through the fabric, and I ached with the pressure of passion building within. I had to bite into my own hand not to make a sound. Ailsa persevered under the makeshift shelter of my skirts, and there was not a trace of tenderness in the way she devoured me. I wanted none. Tenderness would come later, after the first swell of animal need had been allayed.

It could not be otherwise.

Finally, gloriously, the flimsy material ripped under her assault, and she was there, in an instant, widening the tear mindlessly, reaching into my molten core. My eyelids fluttered. A rainbow of sunlight and water, yellow pond lilies and crisp grass swirled about me and through me: months of pent-up sorrow, a lifetime of silent regret. The release I had longed for came so suddenly I would have fallen, if not for the sturdy tree supporting me as I broke apart. A rush of liquid gushed out of me. Ailsa moaned and crushed me to her. She would not let go.

*

"I think you may have anointed me King of the World," she said, later, lying flat on her back under the alders, our coats spread beneath us.

I had my cheek to her bosom, my ear pressed to the throb of her heart. We would have to go back. It would be time for luncheon, and someone would be sent looking for us; Mary would be applied to and would remember, surely, our proposed walk about the grounds.

I sighed and looked up at Ailsa. Her face and hair bore faint but irrefutable traces of our lovemaking. There were streaks down her chin and neck, stains from my effusions on the lining of her gown.

"You're not fit to be seen, Ailsa Reid."

Her eyes gleamed. She tucked a lock of my hair back behind my ear.

"Nor you, Lucas. And yet I have never felt more beautiful. Will you help me make myself tidy?"

"I am at your service, madam."

I rose and went over to the pond to dip my handkerchief in the water. As I lifted my eyes, I noticed that the yellow bulb of the lily had come into bloom.

*

After we had said our goodnights to my mother and father, to Tom and to Maria, who was sitting up in her bed, cheerfully partaking of her first cooked meal in Heaven knows how long, I led Ailsa up the stairs and to her room, sneaking in after her like a disobedient girl.

Fully clothed, I lay in her arms on her bed, and I told her—not everything, but much. I could not bear telling her that her Lilly had been responsible for bringing her fiendish cousin to Bath, nor could I tell her of the poison, if indeed it were such, that had doomed the maid's soul to the Eternal Flames. Instead, I told Ailsa of the promise I had made and the real regret I felt at having been an obstacle to that complete blessing at the deathbed of her adoptive mother (for such she must be termed), which was her due. I told her that I had for some time suspected that Lilly knew something of what passed between us, and that she resented it, rightfully, on account of Ailsa's immortal soul.

Ailsa silenced me with a kiss. I was astounded by how quickly she could stir me, despite the serious topic on which I was speaking. I pushed her back, my breathing uneven.

She sat up, and her mournful countenance was terrible to behold.

"I am the selfish, abandoned creature here, Charly—not you. Do not you think that I, too, have had time to ponder my actions during the wretched interim that you have kept so assiduously out of my way? You lived a calm, uneventful life before you met me, surrounded by your friends and family, whom you valued and who cherished you in turn. Do not interrupt me," she put her fingers to my lips, quelling my protestations, "I must have my say before my courage fails me. I—I will not pretend that I now, any more than when I first set eyes on you, think your husband worthy of you. If it had been any other man... But no, even had he been the best man in England, I could not. So you see, I would have been always to blame. I have wanted you for myself from the start, and any obstacles to my desire I have rejected, obstinate, hungering orphan that I am. I would have you at any cost, even if it meant the ruin of these kind-hearted people, who have offered me shelter, taken me into their easy confidence, on your account. I have stood by your side as you have nursed your ailing sister, watched you pour the comfort of filial care into the bosoms of your distraught parents, and I have been ashamed of myself, ashamed of my pitiful jealousy, ashamed of my rapacious greed. What possessed me to think I could pull you up by the root threads and plant you in any foreign soil I saw fit? I have brought you nothing but misery."

I shook my head violently, but I could not speak. As I clasped her to me, I felt all the ensnaring impossibility of our situation, the all-consuming vexation, the heart-rending grief. And yet a flame kindled out of the ashes, with this simple confession: she wanted me. She wanted me still. Despite the horror of our near-escape from Bath, despite Lilly's frantic efforts to wrench us apart—at the cost of her own life!—despite of what it would do to our friends, our family, against all reason, all constraints, every hope of being readmitted into genteel society—Ailsa Reid wanted only me.

Throughout our childhood and maidenhood, we swore solemn oaths, Eliza, that nothing but such deep-felt commitment should induce us to take up the married state. Or rather, you made those vows, and I gave my tacit consent, for I knew—even then I knew!—that a flame like that I could carry for no man.

You scorned my marriage for its lack of proper feeling, and you were right to do so, Lizzy. Only, I never thought that I should be given the opportunity to live, as it were, by the light of such a fire. The flame of Tristan and Isolde, of Orpheus and Eurydice, of Romeo and Juliet.

"If I should die..." The horror in my love's eye gratified me immensely, I am ashamed to say. "No, Ailsa,

I was just thinking... What if I die? Would that not, all things considered, be a more bearable loss, a lesser sting, than if I should fly away, abandoning my husband, leaving my parents and siblings with a stain, which, as you know, the world would never allow them to wash away?"

"But Lucas, I could not bear it! Oh, what have I done?"

"Oh, but Lucas would be all yours, forever—don't you see?"

Her eyes were wild; she pressed her hands around my face.

"What are you thinking? You must never, ever, Charly, on any account—"

"Only Mrs Collins. Not Charly, not Lucas, not even Lotty, if there is any possibility... Just Mrs Collins, Ailsa; it is clear to me now that she cannot, she must not live! I cannot go back to her. I cannot live out my days in that dreadful half-life of hers. I entreat you, dear Miss Reid, if ever you loved me: save me from her."

"You've lost your precious mind. Lord bless me! Lord bless us both!"

Again, I shook my head. Again, I folded her to my bosom as a burst of tears rendered her speechless, senseless, for a while.

"Hush, hush. I did not intend to give you such a fright. I should have spoken more guardedly. I only meant—the pretence of death. Like on the stage. I have been Mr Charles Lucas, after all. Could I not be the late Mrs Collins, if but for a few hours, to bring about our escape?"

She cried a good deal more. When at last she was quiet, it was as if my words slowly penetrated her distress until she could look up at me, her features pale and sickly looking.

"That is the most awful, wretched, insane scheme I have ever heard."

I could not help smiling. Perhaps, indeed, I have finally lost my senses.

"Can we make it work?"

She sighed. She passed her hand over her face. She pulled lose a strand of hair from her plait and wound it about her finger.

I kissed the tip of her nose.

"You're a madwoman, Charly Lucas. Fortune favours me still. A woman prepared to plot her own death..."

"Mrs Collins's death."

Something of the old, imperturbable Ailsa's *joie de vivre* sparked in her eyes.

"I am tired unto death, at least. Will you sleep here?"

I blushed. "It is not advisable."

"None of it is. But I shall not ravish you in the night, Charly; you have my word. I sleep better when you are by my side. It will help me think."

"Then I shall stay."

Lucas Lodge
May, 1816

Ever charming Elizabeth,

I will allow myself to term you so here, after having received the most delightful well-wishes on Maria's recovery from your counterpart at Pemberley. Maria grows better and handsomer each time I see her; the roses have returned which ever were known to adorn her sweet, complacent countenance, and my reading of *The Vicar of Wakefield* is now the sole source of dread and suspense in the former sickroom. She is weary of her bed and would have risen before now, if not for Tom's stern admonitions. He may be a very well-educated and erudite man of science, but if he cannot think to attribute the palpitations of her heart whenever he draws near to any other cause than a lingering malaise, I shall begin to wonder whether he is a greater blockhead than heretofore represented by his fair cousin.

And what of said cousin? She, too, is blooming, Eliza. Next to their darling Maria, she has become quite the household pet with my parents, who suppose that they may count her as one of their relations by marriage before long. Ailsa professes to adore Meryton—as you know, always a welcome praise to our mothers. Yes, we have had Mrs Bennet over for tea. Now that the risk of catching an infection is over, she was only too eager to visit the Lodge and pass her judgement on the spouse presumptive of

Lady Lucas's younger daughter. Poor Tom! But, as I assured Maria, if he can weather the storm of Lady Catherine de Bourgh, he is not likely to be thrown by the whirlwind of Mrs Bennet. A little folly in our neighbours one must suppose to be a universal occurrence, after all. I think your father has made a quip to this effect on more than one occasion.

"He has not actually proposed, Lotty. That is to say, we do not as yet have an understanding," Maria confessed to me one morning, when we happened to have been left alone for a few moments.

"Don't vex yourself, my dear. Dr Reid is only delicate enough to wait until you are quite well before he makes you a formal offer."

"But I am quite well! Oh, if he would only let me be up and about."

I smiled and hushed her, but—notwithstanding my reassurances—I was surprised at his diffidence. Their mutual affection is clear to anyone to see, and he cannot suppose that Sir William would oppose the match. Before the war, indeed, he might have had his sights set higher, but eligible young men are a scarce commodity these days.

To alleviate Maria's suspense, I decided to bring up the subject with Ailsa. I found her at her needlework, altering the waist of a man's shirt made from a particularly fine cambric cloth, and was momentarily distracted.

"I do not think," said I, "that Dr Reid has lost quite so much weight as that, even if his perpetual watch in the sick-chamber has undoubtedly taken its toll on him."

"It's not for Tom." She looked up and smiled so radiantly that I lost the power of speech for a while. "It's for...for Charles."

"Oh!" I sat down. "Oh," I reiterated eloquently.

Ailsa fastened her stitches and snipped off the remaining thread with a pair of scissors, which, I recognised, she must have borrowed from my mother. She held up the shirt for inspection. It was a superb piece of clothing.

"You have some nimble fingers, Ailsa Reid."

She laughed and slapped my wrist.

"Do not tease me, Charly—not when I'm armed!" She brandished the scissors at me, and I could not but smile.

"Are you... Do you have an agreement with Charles, then? Will you be meeting him soon, pray?"

She looked askance at me.

"When the time comes, he is to convey me safely out of the country."

"Indeed."

I took her hand. She must have sensed the intensity of my emotions, for she put her notions aside and fell about my neck.

"Only for the journey, Lucas. I do not propose to keep you concealed as a man forever. No one shall know us in Switzerland. You can be Miss Lucas there with impunity."

"Oh, Ailsa, that's not... I mean, yes, of course I shall be Charles for you on the journey. I shall be whatever you like me to be. But does this mean you have considered it, our scheme? Do you think there might be a possibility?"

She nodded vigorously. Her hair tickled my nose; I had to stifle a sneeze.

"I do not as yet know how, precisely, but there must be. If you are willing—"

"I will not live without you."

"Then we shall find a way."

For a long time, we sat wrapped in that comforting embrace, which seemed but a delicious foretaste of what was to come. A life in her arms. That is all I ask for, all I aspire to. It is too much, I know; the sacrifices are too painful, but I cannot, Lizzy, you see I cannot—it must be so.

"I came to speak to you on another matter. It concerns Dr Reid."

"Tom?" She withdrew enough to meet my gaze. "Don't tell me he has suggested another application of leeches? I have told him time and again, no more bleedings! Whatever his books may say, I am convinced it does but prolong her decrepitude."

"Oh no, nothing of the sort. No, I think not even Dr—Tom can think that Maria is in need of any more remedies at this point. She is fully recovered, if she herself is allowed a say in the matter. But she's—that is to say, she has told me, in sisterly confidence you must know, she has said, and I confess, I wonder that it should be so..." I fell silent, ensnared by my own circumlocutions.

"He has yet to make her an offer?"

I inclined my head in embarrassment. Ailsa's brow darkened.

"I am grieved to hear it, though I cannot say I am surprised. Ever since we came back from Bath, he has taken it into his head... You see, I had to tell him something of what had transpired. I believe he thinks it incumbent upon him to... Oh, these men and their misbegotten sense of duty!"

She threw up her hands in disgust. I smiled, despite myself.

"I shall speak to him," she said with determination.

"Do be gentle, Ailsa. He is a good man. And, if at all possible, do not betray Maria's confidence. She should never forgive me."

Ailsa pinched my chin, bringing my lips close to hers. "I can be tactful," she teased, her low voice vibrating across my sensitive skin.

"Oh, believe me," I breathed. "I know you can. But I prefer it when you are not."

Lucas Lodge
May, 1816

This morning, I woke up from the most delicious dream. Ailsa, dressed in nothing but her nightgown, unlaced, her long, auburn tresses flowing down her back, walked across a meadow, the tall, dewy grass caressing her legs as she went, all the way up above her knees. It was an alpine meadow, I realised, as I could descry the outlines of austere rocks and cliffs behind and about her; she was coming towards me where I sat by a clear mountain lake. A nightingale whistled its merry tune. I extended my arms to beckon her to me, and as she drew nigh, my nose caught the smell of her excitement, mixed with the scent of the lilies of the valley woven through her hair. My heart pounded. I looked down to see my own reflection in the lake, but the water was rippled by the breeze. I could see nothing.

When I came to, I almost wept to discover that she was not there: that I was lying in my own room at the Lodge, entangled in my sheets, panting for her. We have not been able to meet in private as often as I could have wished; we must be careful, we must not let the servants find any cause to whisper among themselves, she says, and the pain in her eyes makes it clear that she is thinking of the one who went against her. The one she lost.

I do not press the issue. We neither of us could stand the test.

Upon entering the breakfast room, I found my mother and Ailsa deep in conversation, their heads together, Lady Lucas clasping what she considers to be her future kinswoman's hand between her own. The taffeta of my mother's gown whispered against my beloved's plain muslin, as if to further obfuscate their softly spoken intercourse. It was the most charming scene. It filled my heart with impossible dreams, with a deep, bittersweet regret.

Ailsa was the first to notice me, her features lighting up, gratifyingly, to an even greater degree.

"Oh, here is Charlotte now!" cried she and Mamma turned to smile at me pleasantly, releasing one of her hands from Ailsa's to take hold of mine.

"My darling girls," she said (and it bedevilled me, Eliza, I admit), "I am so perfectly happy. The Lord in his mercy has been but too good to us. Your dear sister— Oh, I may call her your sister, too, between us, may I not, Miss Reid? The doctor, dear, kind Dr Reid has just now begged leave to speak to Sir William, Lotty."

"Oh, Mamma! These are welcome news indeed. But where is Maria? She cannot wish to be left alone at such an interpass."

"No, for she is with them, my dear. You know how your papa loves to make his little speeches. Oh, I am overcome! This morning, I wager my nerves are in more delicate a state even than poor Mrs Bennet's. Lotty, do ask Smith to fetch me my smelling salts! I cannot do without them."

After that, the household was in a jolly tumult. With glowing cheeks, the newly betrothed soon emerged to receive the first felicitations and raptures of all, and a tempest of pointless activities ensued. I was quite overpowered by the bustle, though I keenly felt Maria's and Tom's happiness. Dr Reid cast one glance at me, then spoke a few words in his cousin's ear, which brought her to my side within the moment.

"Tom needs a few things from the chemist. He wondered, as it is such a lovely day, if he might not prevail upon us to take a walk into Meryton to leave his prescriptions with the apothecary? He is reluctant to trouble your father's servants with the commission, as he would not be seen to take undue advantage of them, all at once. And he would rather not, as you understand, leave Maria just now."

I well understood. I nodded gratefully at the doctor and went for my bonnet and cloak.

It was a crisp day without, and we had an easy walk into the village. I felt the perturbation lift from my head a little.

"Your migraine," Ailsa stroked her cool fingers across my forehead. "How could I forget?"

"It is nothing." I smiled and held her hand in mine. "He's a perceptive man, your cousin. He will make the best of husbands, never mind his faiblesse for outlandish curiosities. I must thank you for your hand in my sister's present felicity."

"Do not thank me yet, Charly." She bit her lip, her eyes evasive. "I did not betray your sister's confidence, but I am afraid... I had to tell him. It was the only course left me."

"What did you have to tell him?"

I had stopped. We were at the crossroads, turning back towards Lucas Lodge, but I did not wish to be back so soon. Ailsa stood silent by my side.

"There is a great house called Netherfield Park up that way. You must have heard my mother speak of it. It stands empty at the moment; the last tenant, one Mr Bingley, is now the husband of Jane, the eldest of the Bennet sisters. If we walk up the hill to the great oak yonder, we shall have a fine view of it."

Ailsa looked up at me, ready to oblige.

"I should like that."

We turned upon the dusty pathway. Neither of us spoke. Above us rain clouds were gathering, but I could not bear to part with our shared solitude just yet. My perturbation had returned. Stolen moments. Was that all our mutual devotion would ever amount to? The utter hopelessness of our situation—Ailsa's swift fingers working the hem of Charles's shirt—the tortured, dying curses of Lilly—my parents' and Maria's oblivious happiness in the easy, conventional prospects that lay before her and Tom—William, when he—all, all intermingled to create a perfect storm in my mind, a torment at my chest, a heady, despondent pain throbbing at my temple. We ventured upon the grass slope. Ailsa shifted beside me, the skirt of her frock in her hand, a flash of her pale stockings, which—in spite of my knowing her by now inside and out, every nook and cranny having been exposed to and examined by my roving eyes—still provoked a response in me, a dull, but steadfast yearning through the haze of my depressed spirits. I upbraided myself. I should be happy for the happy couple, not struggling in the throes of indecent envy of their fair future. It was unbecoming, unworthy, unsightly. Furthermore, it was pointless.

Closing my eyes briefly, I exhaled as the first drops of rain fell. I tilted my head back and let them patter down my face. Ailsa wove her fingers through mine, tugging at me to follow her.

"Let's run for shelter under the oak tree. Make haste, Lucas!"

The grass was slippery beneath our feet, and I thought: this can never end well. We will tumble and break ourselves. Then I was caught up in the mad dash, the exhilarating flight, our hands locked together, even as our feet beat a sharp tattoo up the hill.

Ailsa's cheeks were ruddy; her complexion shone with the exertion. Wet locks of her hair stuck to the brim of her bonnet, snaked down her forehead. I was panting, my sides aching, my legs trembling under my own weight. But we were there, safe and sound under the canopy, falling into each other's arms, gasping for breath even as we clung to one another, refusing to let go.

"I won't; I won't; don't ask me to," Ailsa muttered into my neck, as though she could hear my thoughts as clearly as if they had been spoken aloud. I pressed her to me. The pouring rain on all sides of us seemed to encase us in a realm of our own.

*

Later, sated, as we sat leaning against the great trunk of the tree, I remembered that my previous question remained unanswered. I adjusted Ailsa's bonnet, fiddled with her breast-cloth. She leaned against my shoulder. I wet my lips.

"What was it you had to tell Tom?"

She tipped her head back and gazed at me, her eyes bleary, still lost in our moment of clandestine ecstasy. She sighed and shook her head slowly, even as her hands searched out mine.

"I cannot do without you, Charly."

I must have looked as grave as I felt, for she collected herself, quaking, ever so slightly, beneath my enquiring look.

"I had to tell him all. No pretence would do; surely, you must see that? You must understand that for two people who are each other's only tolerable relation in the world, who have been brought up as close as brother and sister; nay, closer still, for there was no one... Tom loves me, Charly. Do not be alarmed; I mean that he loves me as deeply and as selflessly as ever brother loved sister, and as devoid of that peculiar attachment, that irresistible attraction, which is present—which should be present—in the communion between husband and wife. As much as we love and esteem each other, we could never make one another perfectly happy, even had no prior attachment existed. But there is a prior attachment, on both sides. However, his sense of honour, his sense of obligation, of chivalrous self-denial—in short, the provoking man would not see reason until I told him that my affections were otherwise engaged, ever would be, and that I meant to take up possession of my estate in Switzerland and shut myself up from the world with the one person, the one body and soul..." She stopped herself with an emphatic gesture at me.

"Oh, Ailsa!" I felt a last, resounding pang, and then it seemed my heart had gone still, overwrought and worn unto death. "I am happy for Maria's sake. Truly, I am. But you must know that you have sacrificed our one slim chance— Oh, but it was ever a dream, an impossible fantasy... He could never allow it. Not for your nor for Maria's sake. It is unthinkable, no respectable man—"

She sat up, motioning for me to stop my bout of hysterics as she placed her hands on my shoulders and leaned her forehead against mine.

"Allow it? You have misapprehended my cousin's disposition, my love. When I said I have told him all, I meant: everything. He knows of my escape, the true reason for my escape, from M__ Hall as well as from Bath. He knows of Mr Charles Lucas. And he knows that I would never let another man, however much of sibling-like affection I feel towards him, be the master of me. He is not in a position to allow or disallow anything. I am my own mistress. I have fought too hard, paid too dearly, for it to be any other way. No, Lucas, Tom has no intention of stopping us. He intends to help us, if you will but put it in his power to do so. That is his chief concern."

"To help us?" I croaked, my mind awash with incredulity. After what Lilly had done: how could we possibly place our trust in another, and in a gentleman, a man who by the strength of his very profession could have us both committed to... It did not bear thinking of.

"Ailsa," I said, as mildly as I could, my heart breaking with the sound of my own voice, with the words I was about to pronounce. *You must leave me. You must save yourself.*

She shushed me. She pulled me into an embrace so fervent I could barely breathe, let alone speak the words on my tongue. I melted against her. I succumbed to the scents of damp wool, vernal earth, and that elusive, enchanting smell that was all her own.

We would never have Maria's and Tom's gilded future before us. Part of me knew that in rejecting Dr Reid, Ailsa had perforce relinquished the one permissible way we could have kept each other's company indefinitely: as neighbours, as friends, as married women raised above suspicion who performed their daily duties together and slept apart—forever apart—at night.

It was the phantom of happiness and for us, who had drunk the cup in full, it would never be enough.

She placed little kisses along my jaw, her fingers caressing the tender skin at the nape of my neck. I listed into her, into Love made glorious flesh.

"Ailsa," I whispered. "Ailsa Reid, you will be the death of me."

Our deepening kisses tasted of salty tears—whether hers or mine or the two mixed together, I cannot say. We would be filthy and dirt-stained when we got back, hours after the time we might reasonably have been expected. I did not care. I did not care for anything but this: time together, wrested out of the fickle hands of Fate. A pilfered, joyous bliss.

Lucas Lodge
May, 1816

Dearest Lizzy,

Maria is radiant, ablaze with love; she reminds me—yes—of you. Although she will never call herself the mistress of any such grand estate as Pemberley, I foresee a mutual respect and comfort in her marriage that will set their household above the finest house in their immediate vicinity.

I will have her close by me, always. I will have an ally, a sister in every respect, at the dire dinner parties at Rosings. I should rejoice, I should—

I must lay my pen by. No, I shall write: tomorrow, we travel back to Hunsford. What a change in prospects! My sister saved, my love renewed, our dear regular practitioner to be my brother.

My suffering at Ailsa's impending departure— Oh, but I would not have her go without knowing that she carries my heart, if not my body, with her. The parting might wreck the latter, but my heart, undivided, shall beat the stronger in her hands.

A dark and terrible part of me broods over Lilly's vial, locked away in my escritoire. Not a grain of sweet release has she left me. It would have been better...

But here is Mary to help me pack.

Hunsford
May, 1816

Elizabeth,

I pick up my quill to write, although my hands are stained with ink and weary of the employment. But I must tell you—that is to say, I must order my thoughts. It has become a compulsion.

I have written a missive each to Maria and to Lady Lucas to inform them of our safe arrival. I have written to you, the true you. On the doctor's instigation...

But no, I must start at the hour of our departure from Meryton. I will forego sleep; the better, indeed, to add verisimilitude to this dreadful tableau, which—

Two mornings ago, we said our fond farewells to Maria and to Sir William and his lady; Ailsa in particular shook their hands and promised to keep up a correspondence from her abode in Switzerland. Dr Reid helped us into the chaise, and we had not driven for more than a few minutes, during which time he had been leaning out to catch the last glimpses of Maria lingering on the stairs of the Lodge, before he sat back in his seat and burst out in an: "My dear Mrs Collins!"

I must have paled to hear that name again, for he made an apologetic gesture and continued: "My sister-to-be, Charlotte, if you will allow me, madam."

I smiled. "I insist, Dr Reid."

"Tom."

I dipped my head in quiescence. Tom cleared his throat, stuck his finger under his cravat as if to loosen it (a feat that would have been near impossible, if, as I suspected, my father's valet had had a hand in tying it), and shifted his position, crossing one leg over the other and back again.

Ailsa put her kerchief to her mouth and coughed in a way that ill concealed the peal of merriment that glinted in her eyes. Dr Reid shot her a long-suffering look.

"Mistress… Charlotte, that is to say," he essayed afresh, "my cousin is a very remarkable woman."

I glanced at the lady in question.

"I couldn't agree more, Sir."

"Oh, for pity's sake!" Ailsa waved her handkerchief as though she endeavoured to whisk away an annoying fly. "Would you please, Tom?"

He cleared his throat again.

"Yes, yes, as I was saying—where was I?"

"Miss Reid is a very remarkable woman," I offered and felt the remarkable woman's elbow in my side.

"Ah yes, quite right; what I meant to say was I have always known my cousin to have a will of her own, a most fixed, unbendable character, even, as I may say, in the face of ruthless tyranny."

His kind face, which had been filled with consternation to this point, took on a grave demeanour.

"Unlike our uncle and cousin, I have never pretended to correct or gainsay that will, solely on the basis of being—of having the honour to be—her male protector."

I looked fondly at him. Ailsa, too, made a little sound that seemed to signify her heartfelt approval.

"I cannot say," he carried on, reddening slightly, "that I am not sorry to have her removed at such a formidable distance from me. However, as I am lately informed of my cousin's and uncle's machinations and since I cannot offer the protection of..."

He broke off. Ailsa shook her head impatiently.

"I refuse to stand in the way of your happiness, Tom. As I told you when you first went off to study at Edinburgh, and as I have told you countless times since."

The doctor raised his head and looked at me with a small, sorrowful effort at a smile, and I felt a pang of recognition in my heart. *He loves her*, I thought. He loves her as dearly as he loves Maria; I would not have thought—I did not wish to think it was possible, but there it was: raw and undisguised in his gaze for but a moment, before he had collected himself and let the veil fall once more over his innermost soul. Oh, Eliza! The way I once, for but a moment like this, took your darling's hand in mine and bade him promise to care for you always, to love you with all the warmth of a twin heart.

Dr Reid bent forward, his grey eyes entreating me. "I have long been of the opinion that you have wasted yourself on Mr Collins, madam. You have been one of the precious few of our little circle at Hunsford genuinely worth knowing, and I have held and continue to hold you in the highest esteem."

"I... I thank you, Tom," I mumbled. "I could say the same."

He bowed in acknowledgement.

"I could not have wished for a better companion for Ailsa, and I will admit that I watched your increasing intimacy with sincere approbation."

I think I must have been bloodless with apprehension, for without so much as a change of expression, he reached into his waistcoat pocket and withdrew a vial of smelling salts. I shook my head but accepted a pinch of snuff instead.

The right side of his mouth turned up in a crooked smile.

"You have proved to be even more of a chameleon than I presumed you to be on first acquaintance. Your wily flight from Bath—"

"Mrs Jenkinson—" I interrupted, then clapped my hand over my mouth.

Tom inclined his head in agreement, and I sighed with relief.

"You are not naturally deceitful. Do not be alarmed. Miss de Bourgh's secret is safe with me."

His eyes sparkled momentarily, and I wondered if he could hear, as I did, Ailsa's cheerful voice vouchsafing: *Miss Anne de Bourgh likes to have her bottom paddled...*

"Charlotte," he pressed on and extended his hand in an imploring manner. "Like my cousin, I have grown up with an acute sense of the stifling wrongs inflicted upon the passionate soul by polite society. I would not—I could not—send Ailsa on her way without her chosen companion in life. But you must be prepared; there are great sacrifices…"

I peered at Ailsa who sat twisting that poor piece of cloth in her hands. The minutely embroidered monogram of CL winked back at me. I took a deep breath and leapt off the precarious ledge on which I seemed to have spent most of my life up until that moment.

"I would do anything."

His visage cleared. The atmosphere inside our hired chaise appeared suddenly lighter. Ailsa held out a trembling hand, and I took it, with all my heart.

Almost sheepishly, shyly, Tom smiled.

I squeezed my beloved's hand and strove to summon a stout look.

"You have a plan."

*

William is back from church. I shudder to imagine him finding me writing these—these witness statements, signed by my own hand, divulging all that is most sacred, most precious to my heart. And yet to stop—unthinkable, for who should fortify my weak, dithering spirits through my solitary vigil in this house? It has become—but here he is—my key!

Hunsford
May, 1816

Dr Reid has a plan. I must write it down, for the ghoulish details are growing out of all proportions in my head, and I can think of little else. It is an ungodly plan. It is beyond Reason. It may well be that we will all burn in the Eternal Flames for this; but I care not! Gladly, I would suffer any punishment, if but for the chance... You see how I fare in this, Lizzy. I have jumped off the ledge, and there is no rope, not one tangled, half-forlorn root by which I can climb back onto it. I am unmoored.

The plan, then, for all its depth, is lethally simple. Mrs Collins must die. She must be put in the grave by her stillborn's side, and be mourned by all her nearest and dearest. Even you, Eliza. I wish—

As far as the world is concerned, Ailsa will have started on her journey the preceding day. There can be nothing to link the two occurrences, except perhaps a certain forgetfulness of Mrs Collins's, a measure of distress at the loss of her bosom friend, which may, in part, account for the sad accident that befalls her.

And what is the sad accident? Will she take a poison that renders her like to death, as in the Bard's ghastly play? There is no such thing, our resident physician informs me. I will not have occasion to worry that I might, as it were, be buried alive. No, Mrs Collins will meet her end—how grimly apposite!—in a fire.

Tom has already found the poor wretch who is to supplant me. She is at death's door, a consumptive and outcast, destitute of any living relations. Little does she suspect what plans the kind gentleman doctor has for her earthly remains, who has taken her case upon him in the name of Christian charity. He is dispassionate, practical—a consummate scientist. The husband-to-be of my sweet, innocent Maria.

What shall become of us all?

Hunsford
June, 1816

My dear Elizabeth—

Minerva's servant calls anew to her silver mistress. It is past midnight, and we are back from dinner at Rosings Park. William has been his usual ridiculous, ostentatious self; I am glad, relieved even. Though nothing could induce me to stay with him now that our preparations are so far under way, I am grateful that he makes my qualms on his account weigh lightly indeed.

What grieves me, what makes my heart heavy, my brain pain-ridden, is the thought of my parents, my siblings, you. To be the cause of so much unhappiness, to never see you again in this life—and yet. A philosophical voice within me—one which I thought I had lost completely during the maelstrom of these last months— reflects that there is not much difference between this my leave-taking and those who depart for the colonies. Though the possibility exists in theory, they are unlikely ever to set eyes again on those whom they leave behind.

No, it is the deceit that troubles me. To be forced into such drastic measures, merely for the sake of not leaving a blot on the name of Lucas and all those connected with it.

And you—would you give me away, Lizzy? Dare I write, really write—? But no, it would be unfair. Apart from the risk, I should drag you down to the level of concealment which irks my own soul. Notwithstanding this, she is worth it, Eliza. Ailsa and Lucas both.

Out of a sense of obligation, we have told our tale to Mrs Jenkinson. It did not seem right—after her invaluable assistance, after the Sisterhood's efforts to protect us on our flight from Bath—not to make her privy to our scheme, whatever its end results. Mrs J. was charmed, of course. She shrugged off the moral dilemma of using a stranger's dead body to obtain our goals.

"Naturally, there must be remains" was her dismissive comment, turning to Ailsa, "I commend your cousin for his forethought. And no more fainting spells!"

Ailsa simply smiled, and Mrs J. took her hand and brought it to her lips. There shone in her eyes an indefinable something, which made me unaccountably grateful that I was taking my love forever out of her charismatic reach.

"I won't tell Anne," Jenkinson added, as an afterthought. "Not as yet, anyway. The girl has never been much of an actress. Maybe in a few years."

I followed her gaze as it touched on Lady Catherine.

Yes, perhaps in a few years.

As we were about to leave for the night, Ailsa, adjusting the brim of my bonnet, whispered into my ear:

"If at any point, Lucas... Even now, I could not forgive myself—I would never be happy if I thought..."

I brushed my fingers over the bare skin of her arm. She shivered and closed her eyes.

"Never," I mumbled back, choking on the urgency of my emotions. "I would come with you now even if I should cast everyone into dishonour—even if we were to be hounded by infamy for the rest of our days. I am doing this for Maria; I do not wish to mar her reputation just as her life of marital comfort is about to unfold. For Tom. For my brothers. For...for William, even. You do see that?"

She stood back on her heels and turned to cast a furtive glance at my husband, who was taking his long-winded leave of the ladies of the house.

"Yes," she breathed. "Yes, I do see. I will be forever indebted to you, Charly."

"No," I insisted, and could not keep myself from stealing one more tender touch of her hand. "No debts, Ailsa. Only love."

"Only that," she echoed, as Dr Reid approached to lead her away from me. My throat tightened as I was forced to relinquish her for the night.

Mr C. came up to me, putting my hand on his arm with a "My dear, we must not overstay our welcome."

"Indeed," croaked I, "we mustn't."

Hunsford
June, 1816

She is dead!

Swiftness is paramount to our success. The few belongings which I will carry with me must be presented in front of Travis as gifts for Ailsa to bring on her journey. The mauve woollen gown you gave me, a silver hairbrush of my mother's, my escritoire. Travis will be confounded by the last item; I shall have to think of some silly speech to make about how I wish Miss Reid will write me often, &c.

I wonder will Travis mourn me? I have not been the most attentive of mistresses, and my natural reserve... I could wish someone would tend the grave; not for me but for that penniless unfortunate who will rest there, for eternity, under an assumed name.

She could not have afforded a grave of her own, the doctor has pointed out, endeavouring to assuage my misgivings. What does it signify whether she lies in the ground as Mrs Collins or as an unnamed destitute in the common grave of the poor? She will be laid to rest a rector's wife—a station she could never have dreamt of obtaining in life.

Her remains will be charred beyond recognition; it must be so, for our plan to work. It is a dreadful business. I am afraid that the ignominy of our treatment of her shall haunt me, whether her spirit chuses to or not.

Maria will go there, of course, when she is Mrs Reid. And my poor mother and father—

It is true I will not be the first child, nor even the first daughter, whom my mother has lost. But I will be the first to have reached past the age of five— Oh, if there were but any other way!

And yet I imagine, given the choice, this is what they would chuse for themselves. Rather that I should die as William's wife than to be a runaway, an abandoned, unnatural creature whose way of life is such that her relatives, on either side, can never hold their heads high in society again.

A person who has committed an unpardonable breach of common propriety.

Hateful, hateful are the alternatives, whichever way I turn!

But it is too late for expostulations. Even now, before my mind's eye, Tom is dressing the cadaver in my brown muslin morning gown. Tomorrow, I shall rise before dawn and clothe myself in the shirt and trousers of Mr Charles Lucas, which lie wrapped in paper under my bed, to ensure that there will be nothing—not so much as a missing article of clothing—which Travis cannot account for.

I will—I shall write when I can. Although I could not possibly send you word, it is a queer comfort to me, my Eliza, to keep up the pretence that you shall know all my ruminations, every machination of my unruly heart, for but a while longer.

I must wrap up my ink and my quills.

Adieu.

June, 1816

Once more, I hold a pen in hand. I have picked it out of my own parcel, sharpened it with my own knife, dipped it in the ink bottle I purchased from Stowe's only Wednesday last. Lucas's pen. Lucas's knife. Lucas's ink.

You will forgive the near illegibility of my scrawls; my hand quakes and the carriage is shaken hither and thither by the unevenness of the road. Ailsa is asleep, her head lolling against my shoulder, her breast rising and falling in slow, even intakes of breath.

I should join her. It will be hours before we reach the harbour, and from thence—

But I have promised myself that I shall write the last chapter on Mrs Collins, and forever be done with her, while we are still, as it were, on her native soil. Lucas, I think, will not spend much time on letter-writing. SHe shall write fiction. Perhaps verse.

We had agreed that our attempt must be made in the morning: for what occasion could I have to visit my poultry-house—unattended—in the dead of night? If I had been woken up by something, I would have petitioned Travis to ask John to go and see what was afoot rather than go out in search of possible intruders myself. Even if this were not true—as indeed, if you know me at all, Elizabeth, you may doubt whether it would be—these are the types of questions that would be raised by any magistrate looking into the matter.

In the morning, then, this balmy, bedewed morning in June, she was waiting for me, the hapless destitute who was to act my part in the conflagration. She had been dead three days already, while we were hastening to complete our final tasks. As I went down the stairs, just before the sun had come up above the horizon, my mind was prickling with images of my hens pecking away at her putrid flesh. I pulled my shawl tighter about me—her shawl, as I had begun to think of it: the shawl I was to wrap around her before I set her aflame with the candle I had brought in the brass candlestick which I must on no account take with me, as I made my escape. I must cry out. I must not let out my poultry. Atrocious, hellish plan!

The rashness, the horror of it. However, the alternatives—we had been over them a thousand times. There was no other way. I must go.

Despite the chill of the morning air, sweat was breaking out upon my brow. I fumbled with the door. Pain prodded at my temple, but I could not give myself leave to attend to it. I held my candle tightly, my innards aquiver, as the door to the poultry-house fell open at last, and I heard the flutter of wings, the comforting clucking of my dear fowls. I went in, and though I followed Tom's instructions to put my kerchief over my nose and mouth, the stench—the foul, unimaginable stench seemed to invade me through every exposed part of my skin at once. My stomach turned helplessly and emptied itself over my boots, which were not mine but hers: the boots on the feet of the late Mrs H___ of Farringdon, soon to be buried as the remains of Mrs Wm Collins of Hunsford Parsonage, Kent.

I had intended to look at her. I had intended to kiss her forehead as I tucked my shawl around her, as I put my ring on her finger; I meant to pray for both our souls. But I could not, and I shall be ashamed of it till my dying day—the second and final one. I threw my shawl and the candle at the abomination, watched for but a moment as the flames took hold, and whirled outside.

The poultry were in an uproar. I could hardly see through tears. I staggered towards the house, out of my wits; then I remembered Ailsa's admonition, as I took leave of her on the eve preceding:

"Run towards the copse, my love. I will wait for you there. You will not have to do this alone."

I stopped, struggling to gain a hold on my enfeebled mental faculties. Would she be there? Even if she were not; what else could I do? The inhabitants of that house would be out presently, and all would be undone—worse than undone. I gathered up my last resources and flung away, through the haze of pain, tripping and stumbling in the half-light, a ragged despair making my limbs heavy and unwilling to budge.

"Lucas!" she cried out once, and then her arms were around me, her cloak sheltering me, and she dragged me, she half carried me into the thicket, as I became aware of the fire that raged behind me, dogs that barked, horses that whinnied, and—at last—a shout from within the house.

I hoped they would be in time to save my poor Bessie. She was a first-rate egg-layer. I fell among the underbrush and wept bitterly, yet joyfully against the breast of my beloved.

"It is done," she shushed me, rocking me as if I were babe and lover and wife, all joined in one. "The worst is done."

We could not tarry. Although the grim diversion would keep the entire village occupied for hours to come, we could not risk Ailsa's carriage being seen on the morning after the day she had supposedly left Hunsford.

Fortunately, the coachman she has hired for her newly purchased chaise and four is a French fellow who will accompany us to the very doorstep of our new home, eager to return to the continent.

Her new chaise. Our new home. It still seems miraculous to me that she has come into her inheritance, that we should indeed be on our way.

To fend off any further harassments from her uncle and cousin, she has stipulated that an annuity is to be paid them, on the condition that they seek no further contact with her. Her Edinburgh lawyer has signified their agreement to the terms.

Besides, if they should ever make their way to Switzerland—an exertion in itself which Ailsa doubts her cousin would venture upon—they shall find Lucas standing in their way.

For I will be Lucas: at least as far as the outside world is concerned. Only in the bedchamber will the clandestine Charly be laid bare.

My final words to you, my Lizzy, before we are forever parted: I am sorry, and I am, all things considered, relieved. I wonder if you remember your dream, that fateful dream sprung out of your juvenile mind, as you close your little Jane to your heart, comforting her with half-forgotten ditties, as you glance up at your husband, as you commit Fitz junior to the care of his nurse?

Word will soon reach you of your old bosom friend's untimely demise, and it pains me, Eliza, that it must be so.

Just before waking to my awful task this morning, I dreamt a variation of your dream. I dreamt that we set our course past Pemberley, for one final farewell. Ailsa brushed off my coat, tidied my cravat, and sent me out into the morning mists. I approached the house, though I did not dare to make myself known. Instead, I went into your rose garden. There were lovely, resplendent York and Lancaster roses, in full blossom, from east to west, but in between all this floral abundance was an unassuming little rosebush, hidden in plain sight, with fragrant, pink buds, closed like fists around their unspoken hearts. Ailsa's rosebuds—an incongruous addition to your garden of stark and dramatic red and white. I reached out and broke one off, and the lady of the house herself stood before me. You looked as stunned as I felt.

"Charlotte," you breathed, in your old voice, and then, as if imbued with my love's spirit for one fleeting moment, "Lucas."

"Ailsabeth," I responded, nonsensically, and like in your dream, all those many, many years ago, you put your hand to my shirt breast and your lips touched mine.

"I give it back to you," you whispered in my ear, as my pulse quickened, as ever, in your immediate presence. "For her."

L.

Heiligenschwendi, near Thun
February, 1852

Iz—

You naughty girl, I knew you would read it all. To think that the aunt I was named for, the aunt whose grave I have tended faithfully since I was but a girl—

And auntie Ailsa! I no longer wonder that I have met her but once or twice, always with a pained expression upon her, always in a most indecorous hurry to be on her way back to these awe-inspiring Alps.

Well now, my dear, I shall never hear the end of it if you do not burn this package at once. I most emphatically forbid you to make any form of copies to spread among our intimates.

At your peril, Izzie!

I am, your must shocked and aghast, and truly, truly your

Lottie

P.S. And as for <u>your</u> aunt—I know she doted upon your uncle Darcy and was everything that is virtuous and charming &c., but.

See you soon, love. Much as these mountainous vistas do grow on one, I cannot abide being so long parted from your sweet—your thrice sweet!—embrace.

P.P.S. Lady Anne likes...!

About the Author

Often quirky, always queer, Elna Holst is an unapologetic genre-bender who writes anything from stories of sapphic lust and love to the odd existentialist horror piece, reads Tolstoy, and plays contract bridge. Find her on Instagram or Goodreads.

Email: elna.holst@egj.name

Website: www.elnaholst.com

Instagram: @elnaholstwrites

Other NineStar books by this author

In the Palm

A Tinsel and Spruce Needles Romance Series
Candlelight Kisses
Little x
Wild Bells

"Gretel on Her Own" within *Once Upon a Rainbow anthology, Volume Three*
"The Silent Treatment" within *Teacher's Pet anthology, Volume Two*

Also Available from NineStar Press

Connect with NineStar Press

www.ninestarpress.com

www.facebook.com/ninestarpress

www.facebook.com/groups/NineStarNiche

www.twitter.com/ninestarpress

www.tumblr.com/blog/ninestarpress